Divyaroop (De█ in Kanpur. As a █ family during his summer vacations, and the love for the place and the mountains has stayed with him forever. Debu studied at IIT Kanpur and IIM Calcutta and had a long career with consumer products companies in India and abroad as a CEO and an MD. Along with a few close friends and colleagues, he later set up a consulting company.

Debu loves reading, travelling, golfing, and playing bridge. He has been writing since 2018 when his first book, *Journey to the Hills and Other Stories*, was published. He has two grown-up daughters and three lovely granddaughters and lives in Gurgaon with his wife, Devi.

Debu can be contacted at mussooriemurders@gmail.com

THE MUSSOORIE
MURDERS

DIVYAROOP BHATNAGAR

Om Books International

First published in 2023 by

Om Books International

Corporate and Editorial Office
A-12, Sector 64, Noida 201 301
Uttar Pradesh, India
Phone: +91 120 477 4100
Email: editorial@ombooks.com
Website: www.ombooksinternational.com

Sales Office
107, Ansari Road, Darya Ganj,
New Delhi 110 002, India
Phone: +91 11 4000 9000
Email: sales@ombooks.com
Website: www.ombooks.com

ISBN: 978-93-5376-896-6

Printed in India

10 9 8 7 6 5 4 3 2 1

Dedicated to all the fans of Arthur Conan Doyle and Agatha Christie with the hope that this book may rekindle happy memories of reading their works of classic detective fiction.

Contents

1

A Voyage to India

Rudyard Kipling Esq.
Bateman's,
Burwash,
East Sussex, England

13 November 1909

Dear Mr Kipling,

Thank you so much for your kind letter on the birth of my daughter. Both Olivia and the baby are doing well, and as the winter season is starting, the little one is becoming more delightful every day.

I have now been moved to Dehradun and have taken over as the local correspondent for the *Frontier* newspaper. I still remember the old days when you were also working with the *Frontier*. I have learnt all that I know about being a reporter from you and I am grateful for that.

We were fortunate to find a bungalow for rent on Rajpur Road with a nice garden. It has several litchi trees and a lovely view of the Mussoorie hills from the back garden. Initially, work was quite slow compared with Lucknow, but lately there have been some sensational doings in these parts. That brings me to one of the reasons for writing to you. A very puzzling murder has been committed in Mussoorie at the Lexton Plaza Hotel and I have spent many days with the police there who are quite baffled. Briefly, the principal facts are as follows.

(A concise summary of the facts so far was provided by the writer.)

Let me know if I can send you more details. I am sure you will find it intriguing and, with your vast experience, would be able to shed some light on this very mysterious matter.

Yours sincerely,
Charles Harewood

***

Charles Harewood Esq.
Ashridge
Rajpur Road
Dehradun
United Provinces
India

23 December 1909

Dear Harewood,

I am in receipt of your remarkably interesting letter. The case does sound very intriguing and I would be delighted to hear about it in more detail. There have been some articles about it in the English press, but they seem to have focused only on the sensational aspects rather than the facts. The whole idea of a murder in a locked room, almost by suggestion, as it were, seems to be quite unique.

I think my friend Arthur Conan Doyle would be very curious to know the details. As you may know, apart from being the creator of Sherlock Holmes, he has solved a few real-life mysteries himself. I will write to him after hearing the full story from you. The flavour of the occult and seances will also whet his appetite.

Wishing you and your family a Merry Christmas and a Happy New Year.

Awaiting more details,
Rudyard Kipling

***

Charles Harewood wrote a series of letters to Rudyard Kipling as the 'Mussoorie Murder' case unfolded. The sequence of events that he narrated was as follows.

Margaret Maynard-Liddell was thirty years old in 1891 when she booked a passage to India. While the first bloom of youth had faded, she was a strikingly beautiful woman. A strong visage, tall with a good carriage and impeccable dress sense, Margaret stood out in any gathering. It was a sad and troubled time for her, as her father had recently died. Yet, there was a glow of anticipation of happier times to come as she boarded the ship for the three-week voyage to Bombay. She had only her maid, Louise, for company. Margaret had met Henry Davies when he had come to England on home leave the previous year. Henry was an assistant superintendent in the Indian Imperial Police based at Lucknow in the United Provinces. He was a fine figure of a man, tall, with broad shoulders and a tanned, smiling clean-shaven face. Margaret was the second of five children—the pack included an older boy, Colin, who had been adopted by the family, as his parents had passed away, two girls, and another boy, who was the youngest. Their father was well off, if not precisely wealthy, and the family counted themselves amongst the landed gentry of Yorkshire. Margaret had met Henry at a ball hosted by the local squire. Henry was almost at the end of his leave when they had met, but he was a quick, forthright man and the romance blossomed rapidly. The couple agreed to correspond, with her parents' blessings, after Henry went back to India to resume his duties. Henry was an orphan with only an elder brother who also lived in Lucknow. Soon afterwards, Margaret's father, George, died after a brief illness, leaving the household to manage on their own.

Henry's letter on hearing the news of her bereavement warmed Margaret's heart. He reaffirmed his love and commitment to her in no uncertain terms, and so within a short space of time, she found herself on the *SS Britannia* in a second-class cabin bound for Bombay. She read and reread

Henry's loving letter during the long sea voyage that finally ended at Ballard Pier in Bombay one morning in September. The weather was warm and muggy, though the monsoon had by and large withdrawn. She disembarked with a crowd of people who got into tongas with their luggage. The fortunate few who had relatives or friends in Bombay waved to the others who went to Simpson's Hotel to stay in the city and to those who went to catch a train to the Ballard Pier Station or Victoria Terminus. Margaret's train for Jhansi was to leave in the evening from Victoria Terminus, so she went there in a tonga with Louise and the luggage.

She had telegraphed ahead for her tickets and reservation, so there was no problem in obtaining a first-class compartment on the train to Jhansi, where they had to change. She finally reached Lucknow after a long, hot, and exhausting journey. The smoke from the engine and the all-pervading dust seemed to cling to her in spite of all her efforts. She had managed to wash her hands and face in the small bathroom attached to her compartment as the train steamed into the Lucknow station. The press of people, smells, colours, and noises was frightening and exhilarating at the same time as she and Louise got off onto the heaving platform. Two coolies had already taken charge of her luggage by the time she saw her friends, James and Emily Sandford, threading their way towards them. She gave a cry of relief and fell into the arms of her older friend from Yorkshire. She shook hands with James, a major in the army, who whisked the entourage out of the station into the relative calm of a horse-drawn carriage. Soon the carriage was moving sedately through the leafy environs of the Lucknow Cantonment towards James's comfortable bungalow.

Emily, too, belonged to Yorkshire and her family had known the Maynard-Liddells for years. She had been surprised to receive Margaret's agitated letter written soon after her father's death but had readily agreed to her request to stay with the Sandfords on her visit to Lucknow. As she put it to her amiable husband, 'It will be wonderful to receive a visitor from home.' The wistfulness was plain in her voice as she had not been away from India for over seven years due to the birth of her children. The European community in Lucknow was close knit and Henry Davies was a popular young man whom the Sandfords knew well. Emily had laughed at the 'strictest confidence' which Margaret had enjoined about her budding romance in her letter as the tales of the beautiful north country woman whom Henry had been smitten by on his home leave had already been circulated widely in Lucknow. It was a delightful romance, nonetheless, and Emily looked forward to Margaret's visit with pleasurable anticipation.

Henry called on the Sandfords the very next afternoon. He was ushered into the *gol kamra*, where he sat down on a sofa. Very soon, James Sandford entered, and the two men shook hands. They were still standing when Margaret came in with Emily. Margaret did not have a clear recollection of the conversation afterwards, though Emily always teased her about how tongue-tied she was. The Sandfords soon withdrew, leaving the young couple to themselves. They came back after half an hour. Margaret ran straight into the arms of her friend. She showed her the diamond ring that Henry had slipped on her ring finger while James shook hands with Henry and clapped him on the back.

The announcement appeared in the *Frontier* the next day as well as in the *Morning Post* in London a week later.

Engagement

The engagement is announced of Mr Henry Davies, ASP, Indian Imperial Police, and Miss Margaret Maynard-Liddell of Yorkshire at Lucknow, United Provinces, on 20 September 1891. Miss Maynard-Liddell is staying with her friends, Major James Sandford and Mrs Emily Sandford, at Lucknow.

The date for the marriage will be announced later.

The Sandford's party to celebrate the engagement in early October was a grand success. Most of the military, police, and civil society of Lucknow was in attendance to wish the affianced couple. The lieutenant governor had made a brief appearance and the party had lasted till dawn. It was a great start to the Lucknow 'season' of 1891. The party was followed by a series of invitations for many social events and the young couple were seldom found at home. They found the time to be together on their morning rides before breakfast, sometimes along the banks of the river Gomti and sometimes on the Cawnpore Road. They often stopped for tea at little dhabas, where the dhaba-wallahs were quite surprised to entertain English guests. It was a halcyon time—for building togetherness and for laying the foundation of a long future together.

**

It was nearing Christmas, when there was a bracing chill in the air and the chrysanthemums were in full bloom, that a lawyer's letter arrived from London. The family was having their tea on the front veranda while the children played on the lawn. The butler had received the post and had handed it over to Major Sandford. He rifled through the letters and handed over a thick envelope to Margaret. She opened it and as she was reading, her face changed colour. She silently handed the papers to James and gestured for him to read them too. He did so slowly and reread the contents before handing them over to Henry, who read them through. A wide smile broke over his face.

'So, my wife will be an heiress!' said Henry.

'Indeed. You must be congratulated on your good fortune, Margaret,' said Mr Sandford.

'Will someone tell me what is going on?' said Emily plaintively.

'Margaret's father's will has been probated. He has divided his considerable fortune into two and has left half to his wife and the other half to his eldest daughter, Margaret,' said James.

'The letter is from the lawyer who was handling the matter,' said Henry.

'Did you know about this earlier, my dear?' said Emily.

'I did not know the details,' said Margaret falteringly.

There was a little silence for some time. Henry got up to take his leave. Margaret walked with him to the gate.

'Is there anything troubling you, my love?' asked Henry.

'No, it's just that Papa's bequest to me is so unexpected. I thought that he would leave it all to Mama or maybe leave half to her and divide the other half among his five children,' said Margaret. 'The lawyer had the will with him, and my mother never discussed it with me.'

'He obviously thought very highly of you. I am sure that you will do your duty towards your brothers and sisters,' said Henry.

'I will! You can count on it,' said Margaret as Henry mounted his horse. He pressed her hand reassuringly and rode away.

Margaret walked pensively back to the veranda, where James and Emily were waiting for her.

'You seem quite put out by the news,' said Emily.

Margaret hesitated. Finally, she spoke. 'I don't think my family likes me,' she said in a soft voice.

'Why do you say that?' said Emily. The concern in her voice was palpable.

'They always felt that my father was fonder of me than of my brothers and sisters. His will has made it amply clear,' said Margaret.

'Do you want to do something about it?' said Emily.

'Like what? Should I renounce the legacy?' said Margaret.

'I would strongly advise against that, my dear. If your father has left something to you, it was with good reason and you must trust his judgement,' said James in a grave voice.

His wife concurred and nodded her head. 'Please be guided by James, my dear,' said Emily.

Margaret nodded. Her brow cleared and she thanked her friends profusely.

2

An Engagement in Bombay

The Sheesh Mahal at the Avikanksh Palace Hotel in Bombay had seen many glittering receptions since it opened its doors seventy years ago. As Anahita Bilimoria ascended the grand staircase, the enormous mirror on the landing threw back a reflection brimming with happiness. That day in February 1973 was the happiest day of her life. She was escorted by the hotel's general manager, who was fully familiar with the wealth and consequence of the scion of one of Bombay's richest Parsi families. Anahita was accompanied by her maid, Agnes De Mello, a Goan woman who had been with the family since Anahita was born. It was a warm, muggy afternoon before the reception to announce Anahita's engagement that evening in the Sheesh Mahal, and she had come early so that she could rest and then dress for the evening.

***

Anahita had met Jamshed Contractor in London when she was holidaying there the previous year. She had been invited for afternoon tea at the Azimuth Hotel by her friend Thrity Cumbatta, an amiable Parsi lady who lived in London after the death of her husband a few years ago. Thrity looked like a bird with her fluffy hair and glasses suspended by a black cord round her neck. She wore *seedha palla* saris and her main objective in life seemed to be matchmaking. This was indeed a valuable service for the Parsi community that had been rapidly dwindling over the years.

'It's lovely to see you, my dear,' said Thrity in her slightly breathless voice. She had just settled down in an art deco armchair in the Westend suite at the Clarizon Hotel, where Anahita invariably stayed when she was visiting London.

Anahita smiled her thanks and offered her guest a cup of black coffee that was about the only beverage that did not upset her delicate digestion.

'It's about time you got married,' said Thrity, coming straight to the point. 'I've arranged a little tea on Tuesday. You must come,' she continued in a slightly disjointed sort of way.

'I will certainly come, Thrity aunty,' said Anahita. 'But what has that got to do with getting married?'

'Wait and see,' said Thrity mysteriously, and with that Anahita had to be content, though she had a fair idea of what to expect along with tea at the Azimuth Hotel. This was not the first time that Thrity aunty had tried to arrange a match for Anahita, but so far her efforts had been way off the mark.

Jamshed Contractor was seated across Thrity at a table set for three when Anahita walked into the Azimuth Hotel. He got up slowly as she approached and held out his hand. To say that a thirty-two-year-old, extremely wealthy woman was instantly captivated would be an exaggeration, but Jamshed's rugged good looks and elegant demeanour did make a strong impression. After that meeting, they were constantly seen in each other's company, and she soon told her friends in confidence that they had decided to get married. Their formal engagement would be announced at a reception early next year. It was a whirlwind romance, destined for a fairy-tale ending, and as Anahita sat in her suite at the Avikanksh Palace Hotel, she marvelled at her own happiness.

***

Anahita walked into the Sheesh Mahal at 8.15 in the evening. There was a service entrance, so no one saw her until she approached one of the chairs that had been placed on the dais. Jamshed, true to the clock, was waiting for her in the ballroom, and as she walked onto the dais, he was there to receive her. The guests rose from their tables and applauded as the couple smiled, waved, and took their seats. On cue, the waiters walked out with silver trays full of champagne flutes so that everyone could raise a toast.

The guests lined up to wish the happy couple. Thrity had specially flown down from London for the occasion and was the first to walk up to the dais.

'You are looking beautiful,' she whispered in Anahita's ear after she had kissed her and shaken hands with Jamshed.

Anahita was resplendent in a Halston off-the-shoulder dress in dull orange, while Jamshed was attired in a traditional dinner jacket. They made a beautiful couple that evening as Jamshed slipped a glittering diamond engagement ring on Anahita's finger and received one in return. The formal part of the evening was soon over as the Volcanos, Bombay's premier rock band, took over. A disco dance floor had been created inside the Sheesh Mahal and couples soon took to the floor to the tunes of Led Zeppelin, Jimi Hendrix, Creedence Clearwater Revival, the Beatles, and a host of others. The room was full of smoke from innumerable cigarettes, and Scotch whisky soon overtook the champagne. All the men wanted to dance with Anahita, so she lost track of Jamshed in a sea of men dressed in black. There was a dreamlike quality to the evening as the hours passed. There was a mesmerizing feel to the thumping music and the multicoloured lights reflecting off the large mirror ball that revolved slowly over the dance floor. A sumptuous dinner had been laid out by the Avikanksh Palace, but there were few takers apart from the old Parsi couples who ate early and left. It was almost midnight when Anahita saw Jamshed again. The Volcanos had switched to slower, more intimate music by then and he was dancing very close to a woman dressed in green. As they passed her, the woman giggled and turned her face towards Jamshed. He leaned closer and kissed her lightly on her cheek.

Anahita's arm slipped off her dancing partner and she stood in the middle of the dance floor as the other dancers whirled around her. She seemed to have been standing there for a long time until Jamshed came closer and led her off the floor.

'I want to go to my room,' said Anahita in a shaky voice. By then Thrity had also come up and Jamshed had offered his fiancée a glass of water.

'I will come with you,' said Thrity. She put her arm around Anahita and led her towards the main door of the

Sheesh Mahal. By then most people had left and the band was also packing up. There was no sign of the woman in green.

'I think you are overreacting,' said Thrity in a robust voice. They were sitting in Anahita's suite and sipping hot chocolate with ginger biscuits that the hotel room service had provided.

'I wonder, Thrity aunty. I hardly know Jamshed, after all. He has lived all his life abroad and maybe his thinking is different from mine,' said Anahita in a small voice.

'Of course, it is different! Everyone's is. He comes from a very good family who decided to settle in Geneva, but he's as Indian as you and I are,' said Thrity. 'I knew his mother well before she died of TB.'

The conversation with Thrity helped soothe Anahita's fears to some extent, but a part of her had been seriously hurt by the events that evening, and almost unconsciously a rift began to develop between the couple. Jamshed had his business interests to attend to. He ran a global trading business that was based in Bombay, London, and Hong Kong, so he was soon immersed in work at his Bombay office.

Thrity met him at his office a week later. Some instinct had told her to cancel her trip back to London and she stayed on in Bombay at her brother's flat on Nepean Sea Road. She had walked in unannounced, without an appointment, so the slightly harassed receptionist showed her into a small conference room adjoining the reception. After almost half an hour, Jamshed came in.

'What's the matter, Thrity aunty?' he said as he walked in. 'What brings you to my office?'

Thrity pointed an accusing finger at him. 'You brought me here. Or I should say your stupidity.'

Jamshed was taken aback by her forthright attack. 'What have I done?' he asked.

'You have had the amazing good luck to be engaged to Anahita Bilimoria and you have immediately antagonized her with your boorish behaviour,' said Thrity accusingly.

'My boorish behaviour? Anahita is overreacting,' said Jamshed.

'She may be, but *you* have to take the initiative to win her back,' said Thrity forcefully. 'Don't you love her?'

'Of course, I do! It's just that I got a little busy,' said Jamshed apologetically.

'That is no excuse. Please go and apologize to her this very day,' said Thrity.

Thrity's wise counsel had an impact on Jamshed. He met Anahita soon afterwards. After the initial awkwardness, Jamshed confessed. 'I did have a brief relationship with Suman once, the girl I was dancing with. She is now married, but we are still good friends,' said Jamshed. 'She is happy about my engagement as she genuinely cares about me. She is very content in her own marriage and would like me to be happy too.'

'Why did you break up with her?' said Anahita.

'We were from very different worlds. She belongs to a conservative Punjabi family that did not like the idea of a Parsi son-in-law,' said Jamshed.

'Why not?' said Anahita.

'I suppose the idea of their daughter marrying someone from another religion was not easy to take. Suman was educated abroad and that is where we met,' said Jamshed.

'Promise me that you will have nothing to do with her,' said Anahita, taking his hand.

'Hmm. That's being a bit petty, isn't it, darling?' said Jamshed. And with that, Anahita had to be content.

Jamshed and Anahita were married in a big society wedding later that year. They left for Europe soon afterwards on their honeymoon and there appeared to be no cloud on their happiness. Jamshed had decided to move base from London to Bombay and when they returned to India in September, it was to be a permanent move. Jamshed had bought a luxurious flat on Pedder Road and the couple moved in there, though Anahita still maintained her family home that was not far away.

Her father had left Anahita well-provided for, and the extensive family fortune was managed by eminent trustees who handled her affairs with zeal and efficiency. Dr Taraporewala called on her soon after the couple arrived in Bombay at her invitation. He was the chairman of the family trust that administered the Bilimoria fortune and had been a close friend and associate of her father, Bahram. He was shown into the newly decorated drawing room of their flat where Anahita welcomed him.

'Thank you so much for coming, Uncle,' said Anahita. 'There is something important that I wish to discuss with you.'

They settled down on the beige-coloured sofas facing French windows that opened on a balcony overlooking the Arabian Sea. A manservant brought in tea and biscuits.

'Please tell me, my dear. Is something the matter?' said Dr Taraporewala. He was a tall, well-built man with a neatly trimmed greying beard.

'Now that I have got married, I think we should involve Jamshed in the family business,' said Anahita.

'What do you have in mind?' said Dr Taraporewala.

'I think we should appoint him as the managing director of the holding company. His business can be merged with ours and there will be gains for everyone,' said Anahita.

'I see. Isn't it rather soon?' said Dr Taraporewala. He sounded cautious and a little sceptical.

'He is a self-made man, Uncle. I think he is a good businessman.'

'Should we not wait for a while? Is this his suggestion?'

'No, we have not discussed this, though he did tell me that there was a lot of synergy between the two businesses.'

The discussion went on for some time. Dr Taraporewala requested Anahita to rethink her decision, even reminding her that he could, as the chairman of the trust, overrule her. Anahita was adamant and finally with some reluctance, Dr Taraporewala agreed to her request.

'I will draw up the requisite papers giving Jamshed financial and decision-making powers over your business. However, it will be a revocable power that the board of trustees can take back at any time. That is essential to protect you from any eventuality. You must listen to me on this,' said Dr Taraporewala.

'Thank you, Uncle,' said Anahita as Dr Taraporewala got up to take his leave.

'I will seek a meeting with Jamshed regarding the merger of the businesses,' said Dr Taraporewala as he shook hands with Anahita.

3

A Death in India

'I think it's time that you started thinking about a date for the wedding,' said Emily.

'Henry is so busy! We never seem to get time for a serious discussion,' said Margaret. 'He just told me yesterday that he may have to go to Agra for some operation.'

The month of February is cold in Lucknow, but the winter sun is balmy, so the ladies were sitting on the lawn with their embroidery after lunch while the children played with their ayahs in attendance.

After the receipt of the momentous letter from the lawyer, Margaret had written to her mother and received a letter in reply. Her mother had reassured her that she did not carry any sense of grievance about her father's decision. She was saddened that he had not discussed it even with her, but perhaps he had relied on her good sense and judgement to understand what he had done. Her mother's letter sounded a little incoherent and rambling, but Margaret took comfort in the main point. The family was comfortable in their Yorkshire home.

Her mother had her hands full with managing the household and had written regretfully that she would not be able to attend her eldest daughter's wedding. Margaret had been a little tearful and morose after receiving her mother's letter.

'I do hope the wretched legacy is not the reason for her not coming,' said Margaret.

'I very much doubt it,' said Emily robustly. 'She must be very busy looking after four grown-up children.'

'Yes, I suppose that must be the reason,' said Margaret doubtfully.

'Of course, it is! You must not dwell on these things when you have so much to look forward to, my dear,' said Emily. 'And just to remove all doubts from your mind, in case you have any, we are your family here.'

'Thank you so very much, you have been such a support to me,' said Margaret tearfully.

'Now dry your eyes. See here is Henry, coming to see you. I will ask for some tea,' said Emily as she saw the tall, familiar figure striding across the lawn. 'Remember to talk about the wedding date today.'

Emily waved at Henry and went into the house giving the young couple a few moments of privacy. She returned after half an hour, having found plenty of things to occupy her in the house including chastising the cook for using too much oil in the cooking. 'The chicken last night was absolutely swimming in oil,' she said in broken Hindustani. The cook, an old Muslim man, only smiled at her and went straight back to his pots and pans. Emily turned on her heel and slowly went back to the garden with a manservant at her heels carrying the tea tray. She settled into her garden chair and commenced pouring out the tea.

'Well, what have you decided?' said Emily.

'We are thinking of the end of April,' said Henry. 'That will give us enough time to make plans and invite everyone. After the wedding, we could go off to Mussoorie or Nainital.'

'That's wonderful! I can't wait to get started!' exclaimed Emily. She got up and lovingly put her arms around Margaret.

'Well, I must be going. I must leave early tomorrow morning for Agra,' said Henry as he got up to take his leave.

'What's happening at Agra?' said Emily.

'Police business!' said Henry with a laugh. He kissed Emily on her cheek and then bent and lightly kissed Margaret on her lips. They watched him as he strode down the lawn towards the gate with the setting sun on his back.

The next few days went by in pleasurable anticipation of the wedding. The ladies pored over designs of wedding gowns.

'It has to be white or at best ivory,' said Emily, firmly scotching all attempts to look at a coloured wedding gown. 'Fashions may be changing, but this is too much!'

A visit to Chowk Bazaar to look at fabric and patterns and meet darzis was exhausting yet exhilarating. It was a happy and exciting week with so much to look forward to.

Emily came into the gol kamra after an afternoon siesta. A few days had elapsed since their expedition to Chowk. It was late February and the first warmth of the long Indian summer was starting to make its presence felt. She was surprised to see her husband sitting quietly on a chair.

'How come you are back so early? Is everything all right?' said Emily with a sudden feeling of dread.

'Where is Margaret?' said James. His eyes were hooded and he sat in a curiously slumped posture.

'She is resting in her room. What has happened? I beg of you to tell me immediately!' said Emily.

'There is very bad news,' said James.

'Henry?' said Emily.

'Yes,' said James.

'What has happened to him?' said Emily in a paroxysm of fear.

'He's dead,' said James.

Emily gave a cry of grief and horror. Her legs would not support her and she crumpled to the ground. Her husband sat for a long moment and then roused himself to get some water. At that moment, Margaret entered the room. She saw her friend lying on the floor and ran to support her head. Emily's eyes opened and as she saw Margaret leaning over her, she shut them and turned her head away. James came up and lifted his wife onto a couch. He then bade Margaret to sit down in a chair while he sat alongside.

'We have received news from Agra. There was a fierce encounter with dacoits near Etah. Many people were killed,' said James.

'Henry?' said Margaret.

'He died a hero's death,' said James.

Margaret sat as if carved in stone. It was a long time before she spoke.

'I would like to return home,' said Margaret. Two weeks had passed since the tragedy. Henry's body had been brought back and the funeral was over. He had been buried at the

Christ Church. There was talk about a police medal for the fallen officer as his actions were considered above and beyond the call of duty. Margaret would have the cold comfort of the memory of a fiancé who was considered a public hero.

Emily nodded. She pressed her friend's hand and looked towards James.

'Yes, I think that is best. There are too many memories here. I will book a passage and get the train tickets and arrangements done,' said James. He rose to go. Margaret detained him with an arm on his shoulder.

'Emily and you have done more for me than my own family,' said Margaret. 'I do not know where my destiny will take me, but a part of me is here, in Lucknow.'

'Yes, we know that,' said Emily soothingly.

'Perhaps my fate will bring me back some day,' said Margaret. There was a far-seeing expression on her face. The eager young woman who had come to India just a few months ago with a roseate vision of the future had changed into a much more reserved lady who looked at an uncertain future.

'This will always be your home,' said Emily. There was a maternal concern in her voice.

Yorkshire weather was bleak and blustery on her return in March. Her mother and siblings were concerned about her, but there was an underlying resentment that was difficult to pin down. It undoubtedly stemmed from her father's will, but it was never overtly stated. They settled down into an uneasy equilibrium. There were beaus aplenty for Margaret after the mandatory period of mourning, but they could not drive away the memories of the broad-shouldered, smiling man in a police uniform.

Weeks lengthened into months and then years. Memories of her fiancé and her father occupied her mind. She came into contact with the spirit world. Mediums and mesmerists. Her restless mind led her to anyone who could put her in contact with those who had truly loved her. She travelled to London but could never convince herself that the mediums she met were not bogus.

'I have taken the liberty of bringing a friend along with me. I do hope it is all right, Arthur,' said Lady Sallow apologetically.

'Oh, that's perfectly all right, Susan. And what is your friend's name?' said Sir Arthur Conan Doyle.

Lady Sallow introduced Margaret Maynard-Liddell to the people gathered at the small flat in Bloomsbury. A seance was being hosted by Sir Arthur Conan Doyle, who had become a prominent spiritualist. There was a select committee of people attending the seance, including a Scotland Yard detective, to examine the claims of a woman who was supposed to be clairvoyant and could summon the spirits of the dead. Lady Sallow was a friend of the Maynard-Liddell family and had agreed to bring Margaret for the seance.

'I don't believe in all this mumbo jumbo, my dear, but Sir Arthur is a prominent man who may be able to introduce you to influential people in the field since you are so keenly interested,' said Lady Sallow.

The seance began with a demonstration of 'clairvoyance' by the medium who was a woman wearing a veil covering the lower half of her face. She was able to correctly identify various objects that the committee members had placed in a locked box. Later, she managed to materialize a 'spirit' that floated over the table.

The committee members were polite but sceptical with the Scotland Yard detective expressing his firm and rather blunt view that someone in the room was an accomplice of the medium. The meeting soon broke up leaving Lady Sallow and Margaret alone with Conan Doyle.

'Do you really believe in all this, Arthur?' said Lady Sallow.

'Well, not all of the mediums are frauds, Susan,' said Conan Doyle. 'What is lacking in many of them is true spirituality.'

'How do you attain true spirituality?' said Margaret eagerly.

'I think it has to do with being pure-hearted and without a selfish motive,' said Conan Doyle.

'All of the mediums I have met so far have some motive or the other,' said Margaret.

'I met an Indian man once in Delhi when my husband was posted there. He was a yogi,' said Lady Sallow. 'I have never met a more spiritual person.'

'India has much to offer. Sometimes I think that we in the West just do not appreciate the true worth of its religions and culture,' said Conan Doyle.

'I have lived in India for a while. My fiancé is buried there,' said Margaret sombrely.

There was an awkward silence. Finally, Conan Doyle spoke, 'I am sorry to hear that. Perhaps I now understand more clearly what it is that you seek.'

'I miss him and my father too,' said Margaret.

As they were leaving, Conan Doyle said, 'If you do decide to go to India, let me know and I will try to help you.'

Margaret nodded and said, 'Thank you.'

She had heard about the Theosophical Society founded by Madam Blavatsky in India and grew increasingly convinced that only by blending Eastern theology with Western occult practices could one truly achieve communication with the spirits of the dead.

**

'I want to return to India,' said Margaret. They were sitting at the dinner table at her mother's home in Yorkshire.

'Why? Is home not good enough for you?' said Colin, her brother, rather sneeringly.

'Hush. That is not the way to speak to your sister,' admonished her mother.

Colin was always the headstrong rebel in the family. He knew that he had been adopted and was perhaps insecure about his real place in the household. He had a nasty temper when provoked and most people steered clear of him. He grew up as an aggressive, rather unpleasant loner, very unlike his siblings. He had tried to assume the role of the head of the family after their father's death, but he was not really suited for it.

The year was 1901. The new century had dawned and with it a new reign. Margaret had been in England for nine years after her return. She was a mature woman now, forty years old, an 'old maid' by the standards of the time. It had been an uneasy homecoming. Her siblings had also grown up. Both her sisters were still unmarried.

'I have written to Emily Sandford and have booked my passage. I leave next week,' said Margaret. She got up and walked out of the dining room. Her mother followed her to her room.

'Don't mind what Colin says,' said her mother. 'You have obviously been planning this for some time.'

'It's all right, Mama. I will probably not see him again and he can nurse his resentment in peace. I can't help it that Papa chose to leave half his fortune to me,' said Margaret. There was a hard expression on her face.

'Are you planning to live in Lucknow?' said her mother.

'Yes. However, I cannot live with James and Emily for too long. I have asked them to look for a bungalow for me,' said Margaret.

'You cannot live alone in a strange land!' said her mother.

'India is not a strange land for me. My beloved is buried there. It is home for me. However, you are right. I will look for a lady to be my companion,' said Margaret.

James Sandford had found a little bungalow for her not far from their own residence in the Lucknow Cantonment, and she soon set up her own establishment. She had several lady companions, but somehow none of them seemed to be the right person for her. It was only in 1905 while spending the summer at Nainital that she met Miss Catherine Levitt. She had taken a suite at the Helen Allton Hotel on the banks of the lake for the summer. Margaret had plunged into spiritualism on her return to India. Sir Arthur had helped her with a few introductions that opened the right doors for her. She had travelled to Madras and met Annie Besant, who was the successor of Helena Blavatsky of the Theosophical Society and had been introduced to prominent spiritualists and mediums in north India. Yet, her quest was fruitless until she met Catherine Levitt. Nobody had been able to summon the spirit of either her dead father or her fiancé.

Catherine Levitt was a tall, lean, imposing woman. She had short dark hair and piercing eyes. She belonged to a good family that had fallen on hard times. She was forced to take up the role of a governess with a family that was moving to India. She had been a medium even before she started working, but it was in India that she found her true calling. Margaret had heard about her powers and sought a meeting with the Richards, the family she was working with. Henry Richards was also in the army, so armed with an introduction letter from James Sandford, Margaret called on their house in Nainital. She explained the purpose of her visit and found a welcome reception. The Richards were quite happy to bask in the reflected glory of their children's governess and readily agreed to release her for a seance to be conducted shortly at the Helen Allton Hotel. Margaret was overjoyed and thanked them profusely.

The first seance was overwhelming. Two other gentlemen from the hotel had joined the ladies for the seance, which was held in a small room adjoining the manager's cabin. It was early evening, and the shadows were lengthening across the lake when they started.

Soon, there were a series of raps and the table seemed to quiver of its own accord. Catherine Levitt spoke in a guttural voice.

'Is that you, Mrs Newton?' said Catherine.

Mrs Newton was Catherine's 'control'—her means of communicating with the spirit world.

There was no response. Catherine seized a pencil and began to scribble furiously on some sheets of paper that had been left on the table for the purpose. The effort left her limp and exhausted and soon one of the gentlemen got up and lit the lamps. The seance was over, and Catherine left without saying a word. Margaret picked up the sheets of paper and went to her room. She sat down at her desk and started reading what was written on the sheets. Her face paled and she reached blindly for the glass of water kept on the desk. The sheets contained a completely accurate record of the only time she had been alone with her father. When her younger brother was to be born, her mother had gone for her confinement to her parents' place, taking the other children with her. Her father had taken her sailing with him when she was six years old. Father and daughter had spent a night on his yacht together. The papers contained a detailed description of those two days including what food they ate and what her father had said to her.

Margaret was overwhelmed by her feelings. At last, she had found the perfect medium. She prevailed on the Richards to part with Catherine and when she went back to Lucknow in September, Catherine came with her. They soon settled down in Lucknow, with Catherine often performing seances that became the rage of Lucknow. In keeping with the times, the ladies spent their summers in one of the hill stations—Nainital, Simla, or Mussoorie.

In the summer of 1909, they decided to go to Mussoorie.

4

A Meeting with Marjorie

The Contractors soon became part of Bombay's high society. Golf at South City Golf Club, tea at the Bombay Club, and parties at their friends' houses became part of their routine. Jamshed was deeply involved in picking up the threads of Anahita's business and merging his own. He travelled extensively as the trading business had offices all over the world. Often Anahita would not see him for weeks at a time.

'If I had such a handsome husband, I would keep him on a leash,' said Sharon. 'Far too risky to let him travel all over the world.'

Anahita was having lunch at the Bombay Club with a group of women friends, and as usual her friends were involved in gossiping about their husbands and whatever else would come to mind. She smiled casually and ignored the jibe, but Sharon persisted. 'He's quite a dish, isn't he? I heard the girls in his office have a major crush on him.'

Anahita left the party soon afterwards, but her thoughts were confused. Had Jamshed actually turned over a new leaf? She decided to visit the new office the next day even though Jamshed was in London. They had taken two floors in Sentinel Building, the posh new office block in Nariman Point for the merged company.

She took the lift to the eighteenth floor and walked into the office at eleven the next morning. The new receptionist did not recognize her, but when she said her name, she was shown into a conference room. There were few people in the office and it was still being set up. The Goan receptionist, Nancy, brought in a cup of coffee for her and stayed to chat.

'Most of the people haven't shifted yet, ma'am,' said Nancy.

Anahita asked to see Jamshed's room and the receptionist obliged. It was a beautiful room with windows that had a view of the bay. It had a large desk and a sitting area next to it. It was quite impersonal though with no photographs or paintings. After a quick look around, she came out with Nancy and started walking towards the reception. On the way there was another cabin, smaller than Jamshed's that looked occupied.

'That's the new manager's cabin, ma'am,' said Nancy in response to her enquiring look.

'Who is he?' said Anahita.

'She, ma'am. Her name is Suman Kohli,' said Nancy.

'Oh, I see,' said Anahita. She's not in office today?'

'She's gone to London with sir,' said Nancy.

She did not notice the sudden change of expression on Anahita's face as she was opening the front door for her to leave the office.

Anahita agonized for days after her visit to the office. Finally, when Jamshed came back from London, she confronted him with what she had found.

'So, you have appointed Suman as a manager!' said Anahita.

'Yes,' said Jamshed.

'Why did you do that? Surely there are better people around. And she is travelling with you!' said Anahita. There was a note of hysteria in her voice.

'Suman is highly qualified. She has done her MBA at the London Business School along with me. Besides, I trust her,' said Jamshed. It was evident that he was not going to back down. 'You are being irrational.'

Anahita said nothing. Her eyes expressed her deep hurt. She turned away and left the room.

Anahita did not really have a family she could turn to. She had a brother, Ardeshir, just a year younger than she who had been a sad disappointment to her father. Her mother had died in childbirth when Ardeshir was born, and her father had tried hard to mould his son to follow in his footsteps. Finally, when all his efforts failed, he cut Ardeshir out of his will, leaving the bulk of his fortune to his daughter. Ardeshir was well-provided for and had more than enough money to live well, even luxuriously, but his father's actions had been too much to bear. He had left their house in Bombay and now lived alone in Poona. Anahita had had no interaction with him for over three years. Their father had died soon after Ardeshir left the house, leaving the two as very wealthy orphans. It had pained Anahita immensely when Ardeshir did not even attend his father's funeral. Ardeshir had not attended his sister's engagement either, though she had had a personal invitation delivered to his house in Poona. For all intents and purposes, the siblings now lived totally apart.

After her mother's death, Anahita had become very close to her father. He had been her mentor, friend, and guide as she grew up. She had been a lonely child as her brother did not provide any real companionship. Her father was the sole beacon in her life. His death had been a real blow to Anahita and now when she was faced with an uncertain marriage and a possibly fickle husband, her thoughts increasingly turned towards her late father. If only he were still there to soothe her with his wise counsel and place a comforting hand on her shoulder! She became increasingly quiet and even her health began to take a turn for the worse. Jamshed was immersed in his work and if his wife's health concerned him, he did not show it. It was finally Agnes who persuaded Anahita to see Dr Gokhale, their family physician at his clinic near Kemps Corner.

'What is wrong with you, my dear?' said a woman dressed in a cream sari with a necklace of beads. They were both waiting at the doctor's clinic for their appointments.

'Nothing,' said Anahita, but the woman persisted.

'You look unwell, but it is the sadness of the spirit that ails you, not your body,' said the woman in a gentle voice.

'Who are you?' asked Anahita.

'My name is Marjorie Richards, and what is yours?' said the woman.

'I am Anahita,' then after a pause, she added, 'Are you an Anglo-Indian? Forgive me for asking, but your dress makes you out to be a sanyasi and yet you have a Christian name,' said Anahita.

'And you are a Parsi. How trivial are these names and how binding! Yes, I am a sanyasi of a different kind and a follower of Vishwa Jyoti,' said Marjorie with a smile. 'I am also an Anglo-Indian. I am not a Hindu or a Christian and neither is my leader. We follow our own beliefs. Does it matter?'

Anahita smiled too and shook her head. 'Who is Vishwa Jyoti?' she said.

'Vishwa Jyotiji is the greatest spiritual leader,' said Marjorie reverentially. She folded her hands and bent her head when she said his name.

'I see. What brings you here?' asked Anahita.

'Oh, nothing much. Just some aches and pains. Why are *you* here?' said Marjorie.

Anahita hesitated. She was a private person and to share her problems with a stranger was not normal for her. Marjorie sensed her hesitation. She leaned over and placed her hand on Anahita's shoulder.

'You can tell me. We are just ships that pass in the night,' said Marjorie.

Anahita started to speak when her name was called out by the doctor's assistant. 'I have to go but thank you for talking to me. Here is my card. Please call me,' said Anahita.

The little encounter had Anahita affected more than she had anticipated. After her father's death, there had really been no one she could turn to. There had been something about Marjorie's voice and demeanour that had appealed to her. She waited for Marjorie to call and when she finally did, two days later, she was overjoyed.

The friendship between the two women developed rapidly. Marjorie took Anahita to Vishwa Jyoti's retreat in Powai and Anahita soon got into the habit of going there every day and spending a few hours in prayer and meditation. Many of the devotees were elderly women who had few family members to turn to in their old age. The retreat was neat, clean, and spacious, but it did not follow any defined religion.

'Vishwa Jyotiji believes that there is no one path for us to follow. We must learn from nature and the people around us and those who have passed on,' explained Marjorie. 'People of all faiths are welcome here, but our ways are different. We do not follow any of the religions. Many of the people here have lost their loved ones and he can help you reconcile with your loss.'

'I miss my father greatly. At this time, I feel alone and helpless,' said Anahita.

'Don't our prayer and meditation sessions help you with your grief?' said Marjorie in a concerned voice.

'Yes, they do. I have become much calmer since I started coming here,' said Anahita. 'But the pain of my father's loss is still intense,' said Anahita. 'Where is Vishwa Jyotiji? Is he not in the retreat?'

'He has gone to our main retreat in Mussoorie. He will stay there till November. Do you want to meet him?' said Marjorie.

'How can he help?' said Anahita.

'Vishwa Jyotiji is a renowned mystic. He has the power to speak to those who have passed on and to summon the spirits of the dead. He can help you,' said Marjorie.

Anahita was impressed by Marjorie's words. There was a deep longing in her and an emptiness that her father's passing had left that was difficult to fill. Perhaps Vishwa Jyoti would be able to do that. Over the next few visits, she asked Marjorie a series of questions about him, and her answers only added to Anahita's growing conviction.

'Vishwa Jyotiji has summoned me to Mussoorie,' said Marjorie. The mediation session had ended and they were sitting in the retreat canteen sipping the hot, milky tea that was served in tiny glasses. 'I will need to leave in two weeks' time.'

Anahita nodded. The need to meet Vishwa Jyoti had been growing within her. Finally, she said, 'May I come with you?'

***

There were many things to be done before she left Bombay for an extended period. Her trustees were supportive, though Dr Taraporewala suggested that she should not stay at the retreat. She could hire a house. That would give her more independence and flexibility. She saw the wisdom of not committing entirely to a monastic lifestyle and decided to take his advice.

The meeting with Jamshed was more difficult. While their relationship had been under considerable strain, Anahita acknowledged the familiar flutter in her heart as he walked into the drawing room late one evening after a hard day at work.

'I am leaving for Mussoorie,' she said abruptly. 'I want to visit Vishwa Jyoti.'

'What! Why are you doing this?' said Jamshed.

'I have been feeling disturbed for quite a while and as you know, I have been visiting his retreat in Powai for some time now. I feel the need to meet Vishwa Jyotiji himself and he is at his retreat in Mussoorie. That's why I want to go there,' said Anahita.

'Are you planning to join his movement?' asked Jamshed.

'No, I am not renouncing the world,' said Anahita with a slight smile. 'I just feel the need to meet Vishwa Jyoti.' She continued after a long pause. 'I need time to think, Jamshed. About us. Maybe we got married in too much of a hurry. We come from very different worlds,' said Anahita.

Jamshed did not ask any further questions. If he was insecure about what Anahita felt about him, he did not say so. He got up and took Anahita's hands in his. She stood up too and he drew her close. He stroked her hair and for a moment, it seemed that the constraints between them had lifted.

'I will be there if you need me,' said Jamshed.

5

Travel to Mussoorie

'We will go to the retreat tomorrow,' said Marjorie.

Anahita nodded. She was excited and apprehensive by turns about the prospect of meeting Vishwa Jyoti.

The two ladies were sitting in the drawing room of Darlington Hall sipping their tea. Anahita had instructed her manager to find a suitable house for them to stay in Mussoorie for a couple of months and he had found Darlington Hall, which was situated just above Camel's Back Road and a short walk away from Vishwa Jyoti's retreat. It was a beautiful house, built on two stories with a veranda on the eastern side. The drawing room where the ladies were seated was L-shaped, with the shorter arm being the dining area. A staircase went up from the same side. There were five bedrooms on the first floor opening out on the corridor that ran around the inside of the house on the first floor. Next to the dining room was the kitchen with the housekeeper's room adjacent to it. In the middle was a lobby area that had a double-height ceiling. A morning room was located adjacent to the drawing room. It had beautiful views of the Himalayas on a clear day with large French windows opening onto the veranda. There was a gravel clearing in front of the house. At the back, there was a pretty garden shaded by a chinar tree. The servant's quarters also lay behind the house. The present owners lived abroad. They had retained much of the original Edwardian furniture but had modernized the kitchens and the bathrooms. It was a spacious and welcoming house.

A bright and warm day in May greeted Anahita as she woke early the following day. The morning sunlight streamed into her bedroom as she woke up to the sound of knocking on her bedroom door. She went to the door, opened the bolt, and unlocked it with the key that was lying on her dresser, adjacent to the door. Agnes came in with a steaming cup of tea and some biscuits that she placed on a coffee table. Anahita thanked her and sat down on a sofa to have her tea. Picking up the empty glass of milk that was lying on Anahita's bedside table, Agnes left the room.

'What a glorious day!' exclaimed Anahita as she took her seat at the dining table. 'I must thank you for bringing me here and that you agreed to stay with me rather than at the retreat.'

Marjorie smiled and said, 'We must hurry as the discourse starts sharp at 9.30.'

The two women were dressed alike in cream khadi saris; Marjorie's beads were the only thing that set them apart. They had been given to her by Vishwa Jyotiji himself, she explained. It was obviously a mark of great favour. Vishwa Jyoti's retreat was beautifully located, just above the road with a large open prayer hall facing the Himalayas. The two women had reached early, but the hall was already filling up. Marjorie led Anahita to the front of the crowd seated on the ground. She gestured to Anahita to sit down and then went behind the small stage on which a takht had been placed with sky blue and cream bolsters for Vishwa Jyoti to sit on. On the wall behind the dais were pictures of religious symbols from all religions. A hymn played softly in the background as the crowd awaited Vishwa Jyoti's arrival. Just as the minute hand of the large clock behind the dais moved to the half hour, Vishwa Jyoti entered from the rear, with Marjorie at his side. The whole congregation stood up and cries of '*Vishwa Jyoti ki jai*' rent the air. He held up his arms for silence and took his seat on the takht. Marjorie remained standing on his right, a little behind where he sat. The crowd settled down and Anahita had her first glimpse of Vishwa Jyoti. He was a tall, lean, and imposing man. A cream turban was tied loosely round his head, and he had a long, black, untrimmed beard. He was clad in a celestial blue robe and had an embroidered cream scarf wrapped around his neck. His piercing eyes swept over the assembled devotees and for a moment, it seemed that he had a personal connection with each person in the hall.

Anahita found it difficult to remember the details of Vishwa Jyoti's discourse afterwards. His sonorous voice had a hypnotic quality and she found herself falling into a dreamlike state. The discourse was interspersed with singing, some of it in a language that she did not recognize. It was not Sanskrit. Hymns and bhajans from different religions were also sung by the congregation. Most of the devotees, as in the Bombay retreat, were women—older ladies who lived in the retreat and followed Vishwa Jyoti as he went from

Mussoorie to Bombay and to his other retreats around the country as well as younger ones who seemed to be workers or managers like Marjorie. After the discourse was over, Marjorie took Anahita to seek Vishwa Jyoti's blessings. She stood in front of him with her hands joined in supplication and her head bowed.

'Do not be sad, my dear. I know you have lost your father and you have nobody to guide you. You are with us, and your problems are ours now,' said Vishwa Jyoti in a commanding voice. He gestured to Marjorie, who came forward with a small steel tray. He took some ash from the tray and smeared it on Anahita's forehead. His touch burned and felt cool by turns. Then, he took a *peda* and put it in Anahita's mouth. The sweet tasted delicious and added to the trance-like feeling of contentment. She bent down and touched Vishwa Jyoti's feet.

'I wish I could talk to my father,' said Anahita wistfully.

'Yes, my dear. In time as your spirit awakens and your mind is ready to face the unfathomable, you will be able to talk to him. Go now and come again soon,' said Vishwa Jyoti as he laid his right hand on her head in blessing.

Anahita sat for a long time in the balmy sunlight. The feeling of calm serenity was growing in her. She may have fallen asleep when Marjorie came up and said that it was time for lunch. They walked to the retreat canteen and had a simple but delicious vegetarian lunch. It was almost evening by the time they reached Darlington Hall.

The next few days followed a similar routine. The meetings with Vishwa Jyoti lengthened and after the morning discourses, Anahita and Marjorie spent many hours with him. He asked probing questions sometimes and, at other times, he let Anahita speak between periods of restful silence and contemplation. She was never very sure about exactly what had been discussed but did have the solace of catharsis with a sympathetic listener. Finally, after almost a week, Vishwa Jyoti spoke about her dearest wish.

'You are almost ready, my dear. You have made remarkable progress. We are ready to take the next step. Next Monday evening we will attempt to speak to your father. In the meantime, try not to think about it. Do not come to the retreat and think of other things. I will ask Marjorie to stay at the retreat for a few days,' said Vishwa Jyoti.

Anahita bowed her head and took her leave. Her heart was singing as she walked back to Darlington Hall.

***

Anahita had received several invitations from friends and acquaintances who had also come up to Mussoorie for the summer. She had declined all of them as her entire attention had been focused on her interaction with Vishwa Jyotiji. Today at last she felt free. She decided to accept an invitation by the manager of the White Palisades Hotel for a reception that Saturday as she was sure to meet her friends and pick up the threads. With Marjorie too away, the house felt lonely, and she was glad to have something to do before Monday.

The car made its way slowly towards the Mussoorie Library and then left on the Mall Road. Saturday evening in May was a crowded time in Mussoorie and the tourists were out in force. The driver was careful to avoid horses ridden by clumsy first-timers, families with their children running all over the road, rickshaws pulled by four coolies, and the usual happy throng of people enjoying the season as he navigated his way past the Standard skating rink and came to a halt below the path leading to the doorway of the White Palisades Hotel. Anahita made her way into the hotel and was immediately surrounded by many friends who had come all the way from Bombay or Delhi.

'Where on earth have you been, Anahita! You simply vanished after your wedding. Is it a second honeymoon that brings you here?' teased Sharon with a chuckle as she kissed Anahita on her cheek.

'Nothing of the sort! I've come here to escape from the heat, that's all,' said Anahita.

'Ha ha! Mussoorie can be pretty hot, if you know what I mean,' drawled Sharon, who was standing by herself at a window overlooking the Doon valley as she surveyed the crowd of men with the professional expertise of a man-eater. Her tubby husband was seated firmly at the bar imbibing whisky with a set of cronies. Anahita moved away a little as a small group of women from Delhi joined Sharon in her pleasurable quest.

The manager of the hotel came up and introduced himself. 'On behalf of the White Palisades Hotel, we would like to extend a warm welcome to you, ma'am. I hope you like the hotel. I would be delighted to show you around whenever you have the time.'

Anahita nodded and smiled her thanks. She had been a bit puzzled by the invitation from the hotel, but she now remembered that Dr Taraporewala had mentioned that their hotel company was looking at buying some properties in the hills. Perhaps that list included the White Palisades. The manager continued, 'We have a big surprise for you today.'

Anahita looked at him wonderingly, but he did not say more other than promising to be back soon. She looked back at Sharon and her gang, who had meanwhile taken to the dance floor with some men who all seemed to be wearing a uniform of sorts with narrow ties, jackets, and shiny shoes. They looked like they had wandered in from a party happening fifteen years ago in a nightclub scene from one of Shammi Kapoor's more extravagant movies. Anahita shook her head at the thought and looked around with an amused smile playing on her lips. Just then the manager appeared again with two men.

'I told you; I had a surprise for you, ma'am! Well, what could be better than meeting your husband by chance,' said the manager. 'Mr Contractor is actually staying with us.'

Anahita looked at Jamshed with a quizzical smile on her face. He put up his hands in a mock defensive stand as if to deny any ulterior motives and took her hands in his.

'I won't deny that I was feeling very lonely since you left and thought I would surprise you by appearing suddenly,' said Jamshed.

'I need time to think, Jamshed. I did tell you that,' said Anahita.

'I will not disturb you. I will stay at the hotel, but I hope you will not ban me from seeing you,' said Jamshed.

Anahita half nodded. She was unsure of her feelings for Jamshed and was a bit taken aback that he had followed her all the way to Mussoorie. She turned away when Jamshed put his hand on her arm.

'Let me introduce my friend, Avijit Sikdar. We met by chance just yesterday when I arrived at the hotel. He was my professor at Oxford. It was quite a coincidence meeting him here. Let me leave you to get better acquainted while I fetch some drinks.'

Avijit extended his hand and Anahita took it. It felt a little cold and dry, but Avijit had a firm grip. He was a tall and lean man, with artistic fingers, and was impeccably dressed in a dark suit. 'It is a pleasure to meet you. Don't go by what Jamshed says. I was a Don, but I gave it up for the rough and tumble of the real world.'

'I've never met a Don,' said Anahita. 'What did you teach?'

'Mathematics. Jamshed was one of my best students. But his interest was only a precursor to his management degree,' said Avijit. 'You need to be more of a dreamer to pursue the rarefied realm of pure mathematics.'

'And are you one?' asked Anahita.

'Perhaps. I think my intellectual prowess has dulled with age and I have become more of a dreamer,' said Avijit. He spoke with an Oxford accent in which the Bengali softness had fused in an attractive amalgam.

'Professor Sikdar has recently come back to India,' said Jamshed, who returned carrying drinks for all of them.

'Yes, my wife died and somehow the prospect of yet another cold and dark winter was not attractive,' said Avijit. Anahita could sense the bleak grief behind the bland statement and warmed to the funny, formal elderly man who held himself under such rigid control.

'So, what interests you other than mathematics?' asked Anahita.

'I like puzzles,' said Avijit.

'You mean crosswords or something like that?' said Anahita.

'Yes. Something like that,' said Avijit. 'Especially if the puzzles have something to do with real people and their problems.'

Anahita's brow cleared. 'Does that mean you are a detective? You go around solving the puzzle of the missing Pomeranian or the maid who embezzled her mistress,' she said a bit teasingly.

'Yes, very much like that. Except that the puzzles are of considerable importance to the people involved. Maybe even a matter of life and death,' said Avijit. His serious demeanour and tone had an impact on Anahita.

'I'm sorry. I should not have made a joke of it,' said Anahita.

'It does not matter. I am so glad that I have finally met you. I have heard a lot about you from Jamshed,' said Avijit.

'Yes,' said Anahita, lifting her brows.

'I do not intend to be his advocate. It is just that we have been friends for many years now,' said Avijit with a hint of an apology.

'Well, Professor, if something happens to me, I trust that you will find the culprit,' said Anahita with a laugh, making her way out of the room.

6

Seance at the Lexton Plaza

Mussoorie had acquired the reputation of being the most frivolous hill station in India. Quite unlike starchy Simla, the summer capital of the Raj, or even Nainital, where the United Provinces government relocated for summer. The presence of a large government contingent ensured that protocol had to be followed rigidly in the other two. Many of the Indian princes decided to avoid the stifling formality of Simla and had moved to Mussoorie. The Lexton Plaza Hotel was at the centre of these frivolous pursuits. Built like an English country house with a tiled roof and extensive gardens, the hotel became the centre of many summer affairs and dalliances. Margaret had booked a suite at the Lexton Plaza for the summer of 1909 with a separate room for Miss Levitt.

The overnight train journey to Dehradun was quite comfortable and the two ladies disembarked at the station to take a tonga to Rajpur, from where they were to start the climb to Mussoorie. They had taken dandies or palanquins and the slow, swaying climb took the better part of the day. Four sweating coolies carried up their luggage and they were quite exhausted by the time they reached the Lexton Plaza.

'I beg your pardon, madam. There is a person who would like to talk to you,' said the waiter at the hotel. He had approached the table in the garden where the ladies were enjoying their mid-morning coffee.

'Who is he?' said Margaret.

'Mr Orson Dankworth is a poet, madam,' said the waiter.

'Aha, that's interesting! Please ask him to come. Also, please bring some more coffee,' said Margaret.

Orson Dankworth was a tall, rangy man with unkempt hair and a straggly beard. He was wearing a purple velvet coat and carrying a little portfolio. He shook hands with the ladies, and if one felt that his handshake was more like a caress, it may have been just imagination. He spoke in a drawl indicative of a good college education that was not borne out by his carelessly worn clothes.

'Orson Dankworth at your service,' said he with a small, affected bow after the introductions were complete. 'It is a pleasure to meet ladies of refinement in these backwaters.' He had a mincing voice and waved his hands a little as he spoke.

'I hear that you are a poet, Mr Dankworth,' said Margaret. 'What do you write about?'

'I write love poetry, madam. I am in love with so many things,' said Orson Dankworth. His eyes lingered caressingly over Margaret as he spoke, and she found herself blushing a little.

'Could you recite something for us?' said Margaret in a cool voice.

Orson opened his portfolio and took out a well-worn leather-bound notebook. He flicked through the pages and then looked up at the ladies. 'Here is something that I wrote in praise of one who shall remain nameless,' said Orson.

Ethereal nymph
With alabaster skin and cerulean eye
Unfettered by coverings of mere man
Rose tipped against the evening sky

There were many verses with innuendoes and risqué imagery, but it was rather pedestrian poetry. The poem was about a real person and that added an intriguing feel of excitement, even voyeurism to the recital. It was a heady mix.

'Do we know who your muse is?' said Margaret.

'Perhaps you do, perhaps you don't,' said Orson enigmatically.

'Is she in Mussoorie?' said Catherine.

'That would be telling, m'dear,' said Orson. 'Can't tell tales out of school. I will write poems about you too, both of you as we get to know each other better.'

The tone of the conversation was distinctly irregular. Yet, Margaret made no move to ask Orson to leave.

'Do you live in Mussoorie all year round?' said Margaret in an effort to divert the conversation to more normal channels.

'Well, I go where my inspiration calls,' said Orson casually.

'Miss Levitt is going to conduct a seance this evening after dinner. Would you like to attend?' said Margaret, changing the subject.

'Aye. I will be there,' said Orson. He gathered up his paintings and left after casting another ironical bow in the direction of the ladies.

'Eight o'clock,' Margaret called out behind him, but he did not turn around.

The seance was to be conducted in the sitting room of Margaret's suite. The hotel had brought in a three-legged, ornately carved ebony table for the purpose. Each leg was fashioned as an elephant with ivory tusks. The table was covered with a red silk cloth. The room was lit with new electric bulbs as electricity had arrived in Mussoorie a few years ago and the Lexton Plaza had installed the new lights within a year. The lights could be dimmed, creating a soothing atmosphere conducive to the summoning of spirits from the past. Margaret had also got into the habit of lighting a few incense sticks, whose gentle fragrance added to the ambience.

Orson Dankworth walked in at 8.30 pm, by which time Margaret was in a fever of anticipation. He was wearing a native Indian dress and held up his hands in apology. 'Lost track of time, ma'am.'

She glared at him but consented to let him take a seat at the table. Catherine dimmed the lights and sat down too. She gestured for them to put their hands on the table, palms facing downwards. Margaret found that Orson had covered her hand with his. His palms were moist and slightly sweaty, and she was acutely aware of his touch. He smiled at her and extended his other hand so that it covered Miss Levitt's hand as well. The seance began.

After a while, she became aware of Orson's knee touching hers under the tablecloth. She did not withdraw her knee and after some hesitation returned the pressure.

Meanwhile, Catherine began to talk in the guttural tones of her control, Mrs Newton. The monologue was focused and heart-wrenching. She talked about Catherine's childhood as a young woman growing up in a grimy town in the midlands. About her father's death and how her education had been cut short. She had got a job with a family with two children, who were moving to Jhansi in India. About her separation from her own family and how she never saw them again. The seance lasted about forty-five minutes, after which Catherine came out of her trance-like state. There was complete silence in the room. Orson got up and turned up the lights. He turned around to look at the two women, but they did not take any notice of him, so he quietly let himself out of the room. The women continued sitting at the seance table.

Margaret felt Catherine's hands on her head. She was gently massaging and stroking her hair.

'You are so good to me, dear Catherine,' said Margaret with a little sigh.

'Hush,' said Catherine.

She continued stroking Margaret's head and neck gently and rhythmically. After a while, her hands went lower down onto Margaret's shoulders. With a little sigh of satisfaction, Margaret closed her eyes.

Orson soon became a fixture at Catherine's seances. She had become quite a celebrity and was much sought after for her seances and psychic abilities. Orson was often her escort to the Mountain Range Club or a private home where she would perform. Not surprisingly, the gossip mills began churning. The poet was clearly disreputable and his habit of smoking ganja instead of tobacco in his pipe did not go unnoticed. He did not recite his more risqué poems in public, but somehow a few selected society ladies still managed to hear some of them. He had had many affairs in Mussoorie, and stories of his exploits became more and more exaggerated. Even the newspapers carried a tongue-in-cheek article about 'spiritual activities in the Himalayas'.

All this salacious speculation made the poet even more notorious but also added a frisson of excitement to their stay at Mussoorie culminating in a grand celebration for Margaret's forty-ninth birthday on 27 July 1909. There was a big seance with eight people participating, followed by a boisterous dinner party. By now, the two ladies were firmly established as part of Mussoorie's frenetic social scene.

7

Spirits in Mussoorie

Vishwa Jyoti's personal quarters were in the top two floors of a three-storeyed building located across the courtyard from the prayer hall. The ground floor was an administrative office, while the hostel for the devotees was in a separate building. Anahita and Marjorie had reached the retreat at sunset on Monday. Marjorie had asked Anahita to wait in the prayer hall while she went to meet Vishwa Jyoti. The sun had set and the last vestiges of twilight were fast waning when the summons came. A peon tapped Anahita on her shoulder and motioned for her to follow him. They walked to the administrative building and the peon told her to climb the stairs to the first floor. She did so and soon came to an ornately carved door on the staircase. It opened noiselessly when she pushed it, and she found herself in a heavily carpeted, candlelit room. There were wall hangings all around—beautiful old Tibetan thangkas. The air in the room was warm and dry and had the elusive fragrance of jasmine. There were no windows. A low, triangular table was placed in the middle of the room, covered with a red silk cloth. Otherwise, the room was devoid of any furniture. There was no sound and she could hear her own heart beating and the ringing in her ears.

She took a step further into the room and as she did a panel in the opposite wall opened and Vishwa Jyoti stepped into the room with Marjorie right behind him. Both were dressed in black robes and Vishwa Jyoti was wearing a heavy silver chain with a strange silver pendant. He gestured to Anahita to come towards the table, and they all sat down cross-legged on the ground. A servant entered the room and placed a tray on the table. Marjorie poured out the tea and they all sipped it in silence. Anahita felt the familiar feeling of calm contentment beginning to seep over her. The servant cleared the tea and doused some of the candles so that it was almost totally dark in the room. There was a long silence. Finally, Vishwa Jyoti spoke.

'Your mind must be totally calm if we are to summon the spirits of the dead. Relax your body and cleanse your mind. Repeat the prayer after me.'

Vishwa Jyoti's sonorous voice recited the prayer that was chanted every day in the retreat. Anahita did not know the meaning, as it appeared to be in a language that she was completely unfamiliar with. But the cadence and the words were well known to her by now, and she joined in the chanting with pleasure.

'Place both your hands on the table, palm downwards,' instructed Vishwa Jyoti.

They all complied and the chanting continued. Now the words and the rhythm were unfamiliar, and Anahita fell silent. Marjorie and Vishwa Jyoti continued, with the cadence becoming faster and faster until Anahita felt her heart beating in a wild, untrammelled way. Then the tempo of the chanting slowed and finally there was silence. She felt the table vibrating, and after a while, it seemed to rise a few inches into the air. She gasped as Vishwa Jyoti spoke commandingly.

'Are you there, Helios?'

'Yes.'

The voice sounded almost as if it was inside her head. It seemed to emanate from a place far away, and yet, it was all around them.

'We have Anahita with us. Have you met her father?' said Vishwa Jyoti.

'Yes.'

Anahita felt a chill down her spine. She wanted to speak, but Marjorie put her finger on her lips in an obvious gesture to stay quiet. What followed was an emotional roller-coaster ride for Anahita. Vishwa Jyoti and Helios had a conversation, with the latter relaying messages from Anahita's father. Vishwa Jyoti asked several questions and Helios answered. There were many details of Anahita's childhood and times she had shared only with her father. She was overwhelmed by the sheer intensity of the emotions that she was going through.

Finally, Helios said, 'I am tired.'

'Yes, you must sleep before the new day dawns. Go now and rest,' said Vishwa Jyoti.

The spell was broken. There was a deep, contemplative silence in the room. At last, Vishwa Jyoti got up. He came towards Anahita, laid a hand on her bowed head, and left the room. Marjorie and Anahita left soon afterwards. They walked back to Darlington Hall in silence.

The next session happened after a few days. Marjorie explained that the seances were extremely exhausting for Helios and that he needed to rest and recover before he could undertake another. This time also, the carpeted room, the tea, and the chanting were the same as before. Helios appeared and Vishwa Jyoti engaged him in conversation. This time, he told Anahita to ask the questions.

'Is my father happy?' asked Anahita.

'Yes, he watches over you,' said Helios.

'I am unsure of my relationship with Jamshed,' said Anahita. 'Should I go back to him?'

'Jamshed is an evil person. He tried to cheat your father in business, but he saw through him. He lost a lot of money because of your father,' said Helios.

This was news to Anahita. Her father had never discussed his business with her, so she had no idea about his associates and business dealings.

'He hates your father. He has only taken up with you so that he can take revenge,' said Helios.

The seance ended soon afterwards, and the two women again walked back in silence.

'I never knew that Jamshed knew my father. He never told me that,' said Anahita at the breakfast table the next day.

'Well, it is unlikely that he would, given the circumstances!' said Marjorie.

'Should I ask him?' said Anahita.

'What good would that do? He will certainly deny everything, and you will be none the wiser. If you ask me, you are lucky to have seen through that scoundrel before it was too late,' said Marjorie.

'No, thank you, Agnes, I don't want any more tea,' said Anahita to the housekeeper who was serving them at the breakfast table.

The last seance was a big setback for Anahita, who had started looking at Jamshed more favourably after he had followed her to Mussoorie. She started spending more and more time at the retreat. Vishwa Jyoti had told her that she should not speak to her father again unless her mind was calm. Interacting with disturbed people was unsettling and harmful for the spirit world, he explained. She complied, but her heart was heavy. The chanting and Vishwa Jyoti's discourses did help, but it was not enough.

One afternoon as the prayer meeting was underway, Vishwa Jyoti left the prayer hall along with Marjorie. This was a normal occurrence and the chanting continued. Anahita continued to sit there, but after a while, her inner turmoil was too much to bear. She decided to ask Vishwa Jyoti to hold another seance so that she could seek guidance from her father. She got up and walked towards the administrative block. There was no one in the office. She walked up the stairs and entered the seance room. This too was empty, so mustering her courage, she pushed the panel in the wall that led to Vishwas Jyoti's private quarters. The room she entered was equipped as an office. There was a large desk with a portrait of Vishwa Jyoti at the back. This room was also empty. She stood there, undecided, when she heard some sounds coming from an adjoining room. She opened the door a crack and peeped inside.

The room was dimly lit, bare and carpeted like the seance room, but there the similarities ended. On a mattress on the floor lay a naked young woman. She was gagged and appeared to be drugged. Vishwa Jyoti, also naked, was kneeling between her legs. His intentions were obvious. Marjorie was playing with herself and fondling the woman's breasts. It was an evil, wanton carnal scene and Anahita was revolted to the core. She had the presence of mind to make no sound and softly closed the door. She stole down the stairs and out of the building. There was still no one in the office when she walked through it to the prayer hall. Her heart was pumping, and her breathing was ragged as she took her place in the assembly and tried to compose her thoughts. When Vishwa Jyoti and Marjorie joined the group about an hour later, images of what she had seen flashed through her eyes and she could barely see through her tears.

'I'm not feeling too well. I have a headache coming on, so I won't go to the retreat today,' said Anahita.

'Sorry to hear that. But if you come, you may feel better,' said Marjorie.

Anahita shook her head. 'No, I think I will just stay at home today.'

Marjorie nodded and left the house. It was the morning after the day of the climactic events at the retreat that Anahita had witnessed. She sat in the morning room and read the papers after a long time. Agnes brought her coffee at eleven o'clock. It was as if a spell had been lifted. She spent a long time mulling over what she should do next. Her first instinct was to report the matter to the police, but that would open a long, unpleasant chain of events and she had no real proof about what had happened other than her word. Finally, she decided to say nothing but gradually disassociate herself from the retreat and Marjorie.

Marjorie returned early from the retreat.

'Vishwa Jyotiji was asking about you,' she said.

'I am fine now. Just feeling a little restless,' said Anahita.

'I will tell Agnes to bring a warm glass of milk for you. It will help you sleep better,' said Marjorie.

The stilted conversation between the two women was indicative of the rift that had taken place between them. Marjorie had suspected something was amiss. A disciple had told her that Anahita had left the prayer hall on that fateful day but did not know where she had gone. Putting two and two together, she suspected that somehow Anahita had come to know part of the truth about the retreat.

'I think she knows, or at least suspects something, Sameer,' said Marjorie.

Sameer Bajwa, for that was Vishwa Jyoti's original name, looked at her appraisingly.

'What do you think she will do?' he said finally.

'I don't know. She did not confront me today, but she may be just biding her time. I think she may be tempted to speak to Jamshed,' said Marjorie.

'Well, her "father" has cautioned her about him,' said Sameer with a cynical laugh.

'If she really knows something, she may disbelieve what she heard in the seance,' said Marjorie worriedly.

'I think it will take her a while to get over the seances. Meanwhile, even if she does not come to the retreat, the treatment must continue,' said Sameer.

Thus, when the knock came at her bedroom door after she had gone up to sleep, it was Marjorie rather than Agnes who brought up her nightly glass of milk.

'I thought I would bring up your milk myself. Vishwa Jyotiji has sent a powder that will help you sleep better. You look tired and I am concerned about you,' said Marjorie as she came up to Anahita's bed.

'Thank you,' said Anahita. She took the glass of milk and drank it in one gulp and placed the empty glass on her bedside table. 'Yes, that does feel nice. Good night.'

Marjorie left the room. Behind her, she heard Anahita's footsteps coming to the door and the key turning in the lock.

The next day, Anahita did not come down for breakfast at her usual time.

'I took her tea up as usual at 6.30, but she did not open the door,' said Agnes worriedly.

'She was tired and must have overslept. Look, here she is,' said Marjorie as Anahita walked into the dining room. She was yawning and her eyes were heavy with sleep.

'I am feeling so sleepy,' said Anahita as she took her place at the table. Agnes poured her a cup of tea.

'You are just tired. You have also not been keeping well. Get some sleep,' said Marjorie.

The next week passed uneventfully. Anahita was listless and tired through the day and slept heavily at night. Marjorie had placed the sleeping powder in a little wooden box by her bedside table and Anahita had got into the habit of adding the powder to her milk herself as her body became more and more dependent on the drug. It was wrapped in little paper packets as dispensed by a chemist. She started going to bed by eight in the evening and barely managed to wake up when Agnes brought her tea in the morning. She spent the day dozing in the sunshine in the garden, coming into the house only when the sun was setting and the chill beginning to build.

'She is quite docile now,' said Marjorie.

'Then it is time that we proceed to the next step,' said Sameer.

'I have got the lawyer to draw up the will,' said Marjorie. 'I will get her to sign it as soon as possible.'

The next morning, contrary to her usual routine of going to the retreat, Marjorie joined Anahita in the garden after breakfast. It was a balmy day and while Anahita dozed, Marjorie took two copies of the will out of her bag and placed them on the table. Just then Agnes came towards them with coffee and biscuits. She leaned forward to place the tray on the side table while Marjorie hastily tried to cover the document.

'Thank you. We won't be needing anything else,' said Marjorie a little shortly.

Later, she persuaded Anahita to sign the documents. It was easily done as by now, Anahita, in her befuddled state, did not have a very clear idea of what she was doing.

8

A Will is Changed

The letter from her brother Colin arrived in the morning after her birthday party.

Miss Margaret Maynard-Liddell
The Lexton Plaza Hotel
United Provinces
India

7 July 1909

Dear Sister,

We have been hearing dismaying reports about your wayward activities in India. Of late, your association with Miss Levitt and Mr Orson Dankworth has been commented upon by many quarters even in public! Clearly, this kind of behaviour is completely unacceptable.

You must return to England immediately before you tarnish our family name any further.

Please telegraph us the date of your arrival in England at the earliest. This charade must end immediately.

Yours sincerely,
Colin Maynard-Liddell

***

Margaret was seething with anger by the time she had read the letter five times over. The sheer cheek, arrogance and high-handed tone of the epistle was enough to make her blood boil. She crumpled it into a ball and threw it in the fireplace and spent a good ten minutes pacing up and down the room. She then composed herself somewhat with two cups of coffee and sat down at her desk to write a note seeking a meeting with James Arbuthnot, a lawyer practising at the District Court at Dehradun who was currently on holiday in Mussoorie with his family. She requested him to call on her at the Lexton Plaza Hotel at his earliest convenience. She then rang the bell and, when the room waiter answered, handed the note to him, asking for it to be delivered immediately.

She then began writing a letter to her brother. It was difficult to write it, but her anger sustained her, and finally when it was done, she was well satisfied with the result. Her resentment against him had been simmering ever since she had left her home and his atrocious letter had finally tipped the balance.

Mr Colin Maynard-Liddell
Village Lower Hawkshead
Yorkshire, England

28 July 1909

My dear Colin,

I am in receipt of your impertinent letter. Your language and insinuations are totally uncalled for, and I am ashamed that I have such a brother. If you have written this letter without Mama's knowledge, as I believe you have, you are completely despicable. I wish our parents had never brought you into our family.

I wish to categorically inform you that I do not want to have anything more to do with you. This is also to inform you that I am revising my will in favour of the one person whom you seem to despise, my dear Miss Levitt.

I do not expect any response from you. Kindly treat this as my last letter to you.

Yours sincerely,
Margaret

***

'I wish to change my will,' said Margaret.

Miss Levitt was out walking with Orson Dankworth when Mr James Arbuthnot was announced later that morning. He was a distinguished-looking elderly gentleman who walked with a slight stoop. He had known her father and had taken a house for the summer fairly close to the Lexton Plaza. Margaret was seated at her usual table in the garden shaded by a garden umbrella. In late August, the monsoon had abated somewhat and today was a sunny day. After the initial pourparlers, Margaret had come straight to the point.

'I see. Do you have a current will, Miss Maynard-Liddell?' said Mr Arbuthnot.

'Yes. In fact, I have a copy with me. The original is with my lawyer in Lucknow. Please take a look,' said Margaret.

Mr Arbuthnot took the proffered document, put on his pince-nez, and perused it carefully. He nodded approvingly and said, 'This has been well drafted. What is it that you need to change?'

'I want to change the beneficiary,' said Margaret.

'Why? In your current will you have left half your money to your mother and the other half to be divided between your brothers and sisters. That is perfectly proper and as it should be,' said Mr Arbuthnot.

'I want to leave my entire fortune to Miss Catherine Levitt,' said Margaret decisively.

'I see. From a strictly legal standpoint, I see no difficulty in that. Your father had left his self-acquired property and money to you, and you have a perfect right to bequeath it to whomsoever you like. However,' said Mr Arbuthnot, steepling his fingers.

'However, what?' said Margaret a trifle abruptly.

'It is an unusual thing to do and may raise eyebrows,' said Mr Arbuthnot.

'Whose eyebrows? I don't care for anybody's opinion,' said Margaret heatedly.

'As your father's friend, it is my duty to advise you against such a course of action,' said Mr Arbuthnot.

'Perhaps then you are aware that my father left half of his fortune to me,' said Margaret.

'I am aware of that,' said Mr Arbuthnot.

'Did you ever wonder why? I did and the only answer that I can come up with is that he had some faith in me,' said Margaret.

'It is not my place to speculate on such matters, Miss Maynard-Liddell. I will do as you instruct me to, but I must warn you that the will may also be contested as it cuts out your immediate family,' said Mr Arbuthnot.

'Well, I will be dead and gone by then. Let them contest it if they want to,' said Margaret. 'Will you undertake the task?'

Mr Arbuthnot got up. 'Yes. It is a simple task. I will have it drafted and ready for your signature by afternoon. It needs to be witnessed by two people. I will be one witness.'

'Dr Williams can be the other. He is anyway coming to see me this afternoon at four for my dyspepsia,' said Margaret.

'I will see you at four then,' said Mr Arbuthnot as he took his leave.

Mr Arbuthnot was true to his word. He presented himself at the Lexton Plaza at four and was shown up to Margaret's suite. Dr Williams was just completing his examination.

'There is nothing to worry about. It's just indigestion. You need sodium bicarbonate. I will write up a prescription. Have it twice a day, after breakfast and dinner,' said Dr Williams. 'Hello, Arbuthnot. Miss Maynard-Liddell told me that you would be coming. What do you want me to do?'

'Please read through the will, Miss Maynard-Liddell. Then sign here,' said Mr Arbuthnot. 'After that, both of us need to sign as witnesses.'

The work was soon completed, and Margaret offered coffee to both men who declined. Dr Williams took his leave.

'I will keep the original with me and give you a copy,' said Mr Arbuthnot. 'When you are leaving for Lucknow, you can take the original with you. Does Miss Levitt know of this?'

'She does not, but I intend to tell her today. Thank you very much, Mr Arbuthnot,' said Margaret.

9

An Unexpected Guest

'Madam, look who has come!' said Agnes. She had walked up to the garden chair on which Anahita was dozing. It was mid-morning and Marjorie had gone to the retreat as usual. Agnes shook her mistress's arm to wake her, and after a while, Anahita groggily opened her eyes.

'Your brother has come to see you!' said Agnes. Anahita looked at her uncomprehendingly and said, 'Ardeshir?'

'Yes! He has come all the way from Poona to see you,' said Agnes.

Anahita half got up from her chair and stumbled. Ardeshir stepped forward and caught her before she could fall. He gently sat his sister down on her chair and spoke. 'Didi, how are you?'

'I am fine, Nano bhai. Just a little tired,' said Anahita. 'How come you are here?'

'Agnes telephoned me a few days ago saying that you were very unwell,' said Ardeshir.

'She shouldn't have. I am alright, only a little tired,' said Anahita.

'You don't look well at all, Didi. Have you seen a doctor?' said Ardeshir.

'No, no there is no need for a doctor,' said Anahita a bit querulously.

'I must insist, Didi,' said Ardeshir.

'What right have you to insist on anything? You did not even come for our father's funeral or my engagement,' said Anahita. 'I haven't seen you for years and now you suddenly appear, insisting on things.'

Ardeshir held his hand up to fend off her attack. He was a fair-complexioned man. With his dominating nose and black moustache, he looked very much like a Parsi. He was rather short though, and perhaps the aggressiveness and rancour of his personality was a reaction to his diminutive frame.

'I am here now, and I hope you will not throw me out,' said Ardeshir.

'No, I will not throw you out,' said Anahita wearily. 'Agnes, please prepare a room for Ardeshir. He can have the room next to mine. Let us go inside. The sun is going down.'

She got up with an effort and did not decline the support of her brother's arm as they walked into the house.

Dinner that day was not a success. Ardeshir seemed to have taken an instant dislike to Marjorie when they met at the dining table. Anahita had introduced them as Marjorie joined the two.

'This is my brother, Ardeshir, and this is Marjorie,' said Anahita.

'Ha, so you are the "God Woman",' said Ardeshir with a sneer.

'I am not a God Woman. I am only a follower of Vishwa Jyoti,' said Marjorie coldly.

'So, what is "Vishwa Jyoti" up to, besides preying on innocent people?' asked Ardeshir aggressively.

'I'm sorry? What do you mean by that absurd statement?' said Marjorie.

'Enough of this! There will be no fighting in my house,' said Anahita in a commanding voice. The effort was too much for her and she fell back in her chair, panting. Ardeshir immediately got up and gave her a glass of water that helped her calm down.

The rest of the dinner was in sepulchral silence. Nobody spoke as Agnes served the rest of the food and the dessert. Afterwards, Marjorie went up to her room leaving the brother and sister together.

'I don't think she is a good influence on you, Didi. I have heard rumours about Vishwa Jyoti and his doings,' said Ardeshir.

Anahita was tempted to tell him about what she had witnessed at the retreat, but something held her back.

'Let's talk of something else, Nano bhai,' said Anahita. 'How have you been doing all these years?'

Ardeshir appeared to be mildly dissatisfied by the change of topic, but he complied. 'I started an import and export business, Didi. I wanted to be like Papa,' said Ardeshir.

Anahita looked at him encouragingly. 'And?' She wanted him to tell her about his life, though she had a fair idea already.

'Unfortunately, it did not do well, and I had to shut it down. I lost some money and Papa's trustees came down on me heavily,' said Ardeshir. His face darkened as he spoke and remembered the implied insult on his capabilities. 'They said that they would cut off the trust's payments to me if I involved myself in any other business. The money was only meant for my upkeep. Like a dole!'

Anahita did not say anything. She was aware of the trustee's misgivings about her brother's business ventures. There had been more than one failure and Dr Taraporewala was close to losing his patience when the last one had collapsed. She recalled the conversation that she had had with him at that time.

'Anahita, I think we must cut off support for Ardeshir. He thinks he is a capable businessman despite all his failed ventures. The trust's byelaws are explicitly clear on this point,' said Dr Taraporewala.

'It would break my heart if you did this,' said Anahita. 'In spite of everything, he is my only brother and our father's only son.'

'The trust was intended to meet his living expenses. Your father was quite clear and generous on this point. It was not intended to fund his forays into business. If he had even a little acumen, I may have been less harsh, but he doesn't,' said Dr Taraporewala.

'I can't stop you, Uncle. You had my father's confidence and I know you have the best interests of our family at heart, but I beg you to reconsider,' said Anahita.

'You realize, of course, that funding these failures eat into your share of the trust fund?' said Dr Taraporewala.

'I have more than enough for myself, Uncle. I would not be able to use all this money in many lifetimes,' said Anahita.

'So be it. The trust will bail out Ardeshir on this occasion, but I will issue a strict warning that this will be the last time. After this, I will cut off all support for him,' said Dr Taraporewala. 'Beti, I must commend you on your love and forbearance. Ardeshir was a sad trial for your father, and he was right when he cut him off from his will. It is to your credit that you have somehow kept up the relationship, however strained it may be. However, I must warn you that Ardeshir is delusional, and I sometimes worry about his mental stability. He has an extraordinarily strong sense of grievance against his father and, by extension, against you.'

Anahita had fallen silent while she remembered the conversation. Ardeshir was silent too. Agnes entered with a coffee tray and served them both.

'If I might say something, madam,' said Agnes.

'Yes, of course, Agnes. Please go ahead,' said Anahita.

It was very unusual for Agnes to speak like this. She was normally a quiet person.

'I am so happy that Master Ardeshir has come to Mussoorie, madam. I was the one who called him,' said Agnes.

'Yes, I know. He told me that you had telephoned him. You shouldn't have,' said Anahita. Her smile robbed the words of their harshness.

'I was very worried about you, madam. That Marjorie and Vishwa Jyoti are terrible people,' said Agnes with unaccustomed viciousness.

'There is no reason for you to be worried about me,' said Anahita.

'Master Ardeshir is your own flesh and blood, madam. I have looked after him since he was born. He cares for you even though your father left everything to you,' said Agnes.

Her words were a bit presumptuous. However, Anahita did not reprimand her.

'Thank you, Agnes. As I said, don't worry about me. I can take care of myself,' said Anahita.

'Well, she does like you a lot!' said Anahita after Agnes had left the room.

'Yes, Didi. She is like my mother,' said Ardeshir.

'Somehow, I had not realized how fond she is of you until today,' said Anahita.

'Of both of us,' said Ardeshir.

'I wonder, maybe she is a bit resentful that Papa left his entire fortune to me,' said Anahita. 'Well, good night, it has been a long day and I am tired.'

'Good night, Didi,' said Ardeshir. 'I think I will read for a while before going to bed.'

Anahita locked her room from inside and put the key on the dresser. She changed into her night clothes and got into bed. A glass of warm milk had been placed on her bedside table. She mixed in the sleeping powder, drank the milk, and was soon asleep.

***

'Oh, for heaven's sake, will the two of you stop fighting,' said Anahita. It was mid-morning, and they were all sitting in the garden in the warm sunshine. Marjorie and Ardeshir had squared off almost immediately and were continuing with their argument from the previous evening.

'I challenge you to prove that there is anything wrong with Vishwa Jyoti and our retreat,' said Marjorie heatedly. Her outburst came after Ardeshir had repeatedly provoked her as soon as they had set eyes on each other after breakfast. Marjorie had come down late and had skipped breakfast as she said she was not feeling too well. She had decided to stay at home that day. 'It's easy to say things without proof.'

The two glared at each other as Agnes walked out to the garden.

'Jamshed sir and another gentleman have come,' said Agnes.

Anahita was quite surprised to hear this. 'Oh! Please ask them to sit in the drawing room. Wait, perhaps it will be better if they came here. Please get two more chairs for them.'

Jamshed and Avijit Sikdar walked into the garden behind Agnes. A manservant brought out two more garden chairs for the visitors. Avijit was immaculately dressed as usual in his tweeds and Jamshed looked very elegant in a grey suit. They came over and shook hands while Anahita made the introductions. After some general conversation, Jamshed said politely, 'I am sorry that we have barged in without an invitation. We had heard that you were not keeping well, so we decided to call on you.'

'I am all right,' said Anahita politely, though she was touched by the concern in Jamshed's voice.

'My brother has come all the way from Poona to see me,' she added. 'I am worried about Didi. That bloody Vishwa Jyoti has got his claws in her,' said Ardeshir aggressively.

'Don't abuse Vishwa Jyotiji or it will be the worst for you!' exclaimed Marjorie.

'How? What will you do to me? Suck my blood out as you are doing to other defenceless women?' shouted Ardeshir, shaking his fist at Marjorie.

'I am telling you to shut up. I am not going to tolerate this abuse!' said Marjorie, getting up from her chair.

'I'll abuse whomever I bloody well feel like! I know your breed,' sneered Ardeshir.

'Are you going to sit here and let your brother abuse me?' said Marjorie looking at Anahita. 'Do you agree with what he's saying?'

Anahita remained silent. After glaring at her for a while, Marjorie said, 'I am going to the retreat now. I will seek Vishwa Jyotiji's advice on what should be done.'

Marjorie stalked off. There was silence for some time.

'I am sorry you have been subjected to this,' said Anahita apologetically. 'My brother is very protective of me.'

'That bitch needed to get it in the neck,' snarled Ardeshir.

Anahita held up her hand. 'Please, no further abuse and foul language. We have had enough of this excitement.'

'I again apologize for barging in today,' said Jamshed.

'Please! There is no need for you to say that,' said Anahita.

'Is there anything that you would like to tell us?' said Avijit.

'Such as?' said Anahita.

'Anything out of the ordinary. Something that you may have seen or heard that struck you as odd,' said Avijit.

Anahita hesitated. Finally, she spoke slowly. 'There are things about the retreat that are not what I expected. They are far from acceptable, to say the least.'

'Like what?' said Avijit.

'I want to forget about the whole thing. I had already decided that I would cut off my links with them. Ardeshir's arrival has only precipitated matters,' said Anahita.

'Would it not be better for you to discuss what you have seen or heard about the retreat with us?' said Avijit.

'No. I think on balance, it would be better to let things be as they are. I do not want to get involved in anything messy,' said Anahita. 'I am sorry I have not been forthcoming.'

Avijit had to be content with that. 'If you ever feel the need to discuss anything, you know where to find me.'

Jamshed got up to take his leave. 'Perhaps it's better that matters came to a head. I respect your decision to stay silent, but given what you have said, any further interaction with this Vishwa Jyoti seems to be undesirable.' He came up to Anahita and took her hands in his. 'I hope you know that I will be there for you, whenever you need me.'

Anahita half nodded and looked away.

The calming influence of the two men was welcome. The day had been eventful, but it was not over yet. Brother and sister sat in the garden the whole day with Agnes serving them lunch on a garden table. They talked at length of their happier childhood days, only going into the house when the shadows lengthened.

Marjorie returned to Darlington Hall that evening at sunset. She walked into the drawing room and came straight up to Anahita.

'I need to talk to you,' said Marjorie.

'Go ahead,' said Anahita.

'Not in front of him,' said Marjorie gesturing at Ardeshir with undisguised loathing.

'Well then, let us go into the morning room. Ardeshir, can you tell Agnes to bring in some coffee?' said Anahita.

When Agnes took in the coffee a few minutes later at around six in the evening, she found the two women talking agitatedly. They fell silent as she walked in and poured the coffee. Later, both she and Ardeshir could hear raised voices coming from the closed room. Agnes went closer to the closed door so that she could hear the conversation better.

'Your retreat is a den of vice and your Vishwa Jyoti is nothing but a rapist,' screamed Anahita loudly enough for Agnes to hear about twenty minutes later. She could not hear Marjorie's response, but after a while the door was flung open, and Anahita literally dragged Marjorie up the stairs to her bedroom.

'You evil woman! You have kept me drugged all this time while you are going about your nasty business!' screamed Anahita. 'I will show you what I will do with you and your precious Vishwa Jyoti!'

Anahita stormed into her bedroom firmly holding Marjorie by her hand and slammed the door shut behind her. Agnes and Ardeshir followed them up the stairs but could not hear what was happening behind the closed door. Anahita emptied the wooden box that contained the sleeping powders and flushed them down the toilet. Marjorie was cowering by the side of the bed. Agnes and Ardeshir were standing in the hallway as she came out of the bedroom.

'Now get out of my house!' shouted Anahita, wagging her finger in Marjorie's face. 'Don't bother to pack. I will have your filthy clothes sent up to the retreat tomorrow.' With that, she literally pushed Marjorie out of the room. Agnes followed her and firmly shut the front door behind her after Marjorie had left the house.

Anahita was trembling with anger and had to take the support of the door frame to stay upright. Her brother came up and led her down the stairs to the drawing room. They sat in silence while Agnes brought water for them to drink.

'I am feeling very tired,' said Anahita.

'I will get some coffee, madam. That will help clear your head,' said Agnes. She went out and returned with coffee for both.

'You should go to bed early,' said Ardeshir. 'I will tell Agnes to put dinner earlier.' He left the room, leaving Anahita sitting on the sofa and sipping her coffee.

Dinner was in silence. Talking was an effort for Anahita and as soon as her sketchy meal was over, she went up to her room. She declined her brother's help in climbing the stairs and used the support of the bannisters.

Agnes followed her a little later with her nightly glass of milk. Anahita was lying in bed and appeared to be almost asleep already. Agnes shook her gently, but she did not stir, so she placed the glass of the milk on the bedside table and quietly left the room, shutting the door behind her.

Ardeshir went up to his room soon afterwards. Agnes cleared up the kitchen and retired too.

The house fell quiet.

10

Death at the Lexton Plaza

'Sophia Richards has written a very nice letter inviting us to Jhansi for the winter,' said Margaret. Miss Levitt's former employers had kept in touch with her over the years and they had become close friends. They were also keen spiritualists and looked forward to welcoming their former governess so that she could conduct a few seances at their house. 'I'm planning to accept. What do you think?'

'Yes. I think it will be nice to visit the Richards. Jhansi is also balmy in winter. Winter there is milder than Lucknow and that will be good for your rheumatism,' said Catherine.

'You are always so thoughtful, my dear. I will write and accept their invitation,' said Margaret.

'Shall I go to Lucknow for packing up in advance and you could follow later or perhaps go directly to Jhansi from here?' said Catherine.

Margaret considered. 'Well, I suppose I could manage without you for a week or two. It will certainly make travel easier for me.'

'Then I will plan to leave for Lucknow soon. The season is already ending here, and the town is thin of company,' said Catherine.

Catherine left for Lucknow on 14 September. Margaret had booked a ticket to Delhi and onwards to Jhansi on 24 September, giving Catherine enough time to pack up in Lucknow and be in Jhansi to await her arrival.

***

Margaret was found dead in her bed on the morning of 21 September. The waiter who brought up her morning tea knocked on the door of her suite at seven as usual. There was no response. This was unusual, so he took the tray back to the kitchen and reported the matter to the head steward. Finally, the manager of the hotel, a Swiss national, went up to Margaret's suite accompanied by the head steward and the head of housekeeping. There was no response to their knocks and raised voices, so he instructed the head of housekeeping to open the door with her master key. This did not work either as the door was bolted from the inside. By now a small crowd of hotel residents had gathered. The hotel manager asked them to go back to their rooms and then told some of the waiters to break the door down. This took a while, but eventually the door fell in with a crash. The manager, along with his senior staff, entered the suite. The ante room was untouched, but when they entered the bedroom, they found Margaret lying on the bed. The manager went ahead and took up her hand. It was cold and lifeless and there was no pulse. He gestured to everyone to leave the room. Leaving two waiters in charge with clear instructions to not allow anyone to enter the room, he sent two footmen with urgent notes for the police and Dr Williams.

Police Inspector Vijay Rathore was the first to arrive.

'What has happened here, Mr Schmidt?' said the inspector to the manager of the hotel.

'One of our guests at the hotel has been found dead in her room,' said the manager.

'Do you suspect that it is not a normal death?' said the inspector.

'I'm not sure, Inspector. There's something about the way her body is lying. It's unnatural,' blurted out Mr Schmidt.

Dr Williams walked into the manager's office. Mr Schmidt filled him in quickly and the three men, accompanied by a police constable, went up to Margaret's room.

Margaret was lying on the bed with her hands folded on her chest. Her bedclothes were perfectly arranged, and her hair and nightgown were not dishevelled. It did not look like she was even asleep but almost as if she were lying there awake. Her eyes were closed and there was an unnatural pallor on her face. Her bedroom slippers lay neatly by the side of the bed, and the room looked like it had not been used at all.

The doctor bent forward and sniffed her lips. The smell of bitter almonds still lingered in the air. He felt her pulse and confirmed that she was indeed dead.

The policemen examined the room. On the bedside table there was a bottle labelled 'sodium bicarbonate' and an empty glass stained with milk.

'I will have to call in Captain Willoughby,' said Dr Williams. The inspector nodded. Captain Willoughby was the civil surgeon in Mussoorie. He relieved the waiters who had been guarding the room and placed the constable there. The three men then walked back to the manager's office.

The inspector sent an urgent telegram to his superior, the Assistant Superintendent of Police (ASP), Mr Carrington, in Dehradun, and a note was sent to Captain Willoughby asking him to come immediately. The inspector asked for the use of a private office and requested the manager to send in people one by one for questioning. A small contingent of constables had also come to the hotel by then to assist the inspector. The first person to be questioned was Louise, Margaret's maid. She was staying in the servant's wing at the back of the hotel. She confirmed that her mistress had been in good health and spirits. Similar views were expressed by the manager and other staff who had met Margaret.

One of the ayahs working with another family staying at the hotel told the inspector that she had not slept well the previous night. She said that she had seen a person walking on the roof of the hotel, but she could not make out anything else as the night was too dark. Her evidence was considered fanciful, and the inspector chose to disregard it.

Captain Willoughby decided to conduct an autopsy, given the puzzling circumstances of the case. It was duly found that Margaret had died of poisoning by prussic acid. That accounted for the smell of bitter almonds around her lips. There was no trace of poison in the bottle of sodium bicarbonate or on the glass that had been found on her bedside table. A thorough search of her room failed to find any trace of the poison anywhere. Other than that, there was also nothing incriminating at all. The suite was accessed via a door opening from the sitting room onto the hotel corridor. This was the door that had been broken down by the hotel staff. There was also a skylight with a small opening on the roof in the sitting room, but it was high and inaccessible. There were windows opening out towards the mountains in both the sitting room as well as the bedroom, but there was a sheer drop to the parapet below and the walls were unclimbable. For all intents and purposes, Margaret's suite was impenetrable.

Captain Willoughby, Dr Williams, and Mr Carrington met at the Lexton Plaza Hotel a few days later to discuss the case.

'Prussic acid is a very quick acting poison, Dr Williams,' said Captain Willoughby.

'I am aware of that,' said Dr Williams.

'Since she was lying on her back, seemingly undisturbed, would you say it's possible that she ingested the poison and then lay down on the bed?' said Captain Willoughby.

'Unlikely, I would say. She would have got into some kind of spasm,' said Dr Williams.

'So, someone gave her the poison as she slept,' said Captain Willoughby.

'The key questions remain. How did the murderer get in and get out? How did he administer the poison?' said the ASP, who had come in from Dehradun to take charge of the case.

'He or she?' murmured the captain.

'Indeed. The only problem is that "she" was not in Mussoorie, but in Lucknow. There are innumerable witnesses to testify to that,' said the ASP. There was no question of misunderstanding who the "she" was. 'Frankly, we are none the wiser, gentlemen.'

'Murder by suggestion,' said Dr Williams. He was reading a headline from the *Sentinel*, a newspaper published from Mussoorie.

'Tchah,' said Captain Willoughby forcefully. 'We are in the twentieth century, gentlemen, and there is no room for such claptrap.'

'Well, hypnotic suggestion has been known to happen. Also, what do you think of this seance business?' said the ASP.

'Well, I think the only possibilities are that someone either managed to get into the room and administer the poison or the victim ingested the poison on her own,' said the captain.

'True enough, but how did someone get in? And why are there no traces of prussic acid anywhere?' said Dr Williams.

'I don't think we are getting anywhere. We seem to be going round in circles,' said the ASP.

Mussoorie social circles were abuzz with feverish talk and gossip about the inexplicable murder at the Lexton Plaza. Popular opinion had turned strongly against Miss Catherine Levitt. Talk of their bohemian lifestyle, the seances, the occult, spiritualism, and their association with unsavoury characters like Orson Dankworth had reached a fever pitch. Miss Levitt had returned to Mussoorie but was not staying at the Lexton Plaza. She chose a smaller hotel nearby instead. She had attended Margaret's funeral but was ignored socially by most people.

The police were making no progress in the case as the ASP had been forced to admit to the civil surgeon and Dr Williams.

11

A Mysterious Murder

A little after the inhabitants of Darlington Hall had gone to sleep that night, there was a loud crash. This came to light during the police investigations that took place the next day.

'I think I had just gone to sleep when I heard a loud crash. It sounded like a table had fallen over. There was also the sound of breaking glass. It sounded really loud in the quiet night,' said Agnes.

'It was my bedside table that fell over. I got up to go to the bathroom and tripped over it. It fell and the tray with the bottle of water and the glass fell and broke. The bedside lamp broke as well. It made a very loud noise, and I thought that people would wake up, but as nobody did, I went back to sleep,' said Ardeshir.

At 6.30 that morning, Agnes carried up Anahita's bed tea. She knocked on her door and, upon receiving no response, tried to open it, but it was locked. She knocked again more loudly and called Anahita's name as well. Finally, when there was still no response, she took the tea tray back to the kitchen.

'It's very strange. I have never known madam to sleep like this,' said Agnes to Parvati, the cook. 'This is the second time she is sleeping so late.'

Parvati's husband, Ram Singh, was Anahita's driver. Along with Gyan Chand, the gardener, and Albert, the Goan bearer, they comprised the domestic staff at Darlington Hall. Morning tea was a ritual with all the staff, and they were all present when Agnes came back down with the tea tray.

'Madam has not been well lately. I hope she is all right,' said Ram Singh.

Just then Ardeshir walked into the kitchen wearing a dressing gown over his pyjamas and carpet slippers.

'What's going on here? Agnes, I heard you knocking at Didi's door and calling out her name. What's the matter?' said Ardeshir.

Agnes explained what had happened. Ardeshir decided to go up to Anahita's room to see for himself. He was followed by the entire staff. He knocked on Anahita's door, but there was no answer. He tried the handle, but the door was locked from inside just as Agnes had told him.

'I am worried about this. We must break the door down,' said Ardeshir. He told the gardener and the driver to push the door with their shoulders. It took a while but suddenly the door hinges gave way and the door fell inwards with a loud crash. Ardeshir entered the room followed by the servants. Agnes was the last to come into the room.

Anahita was lying on her bed on her back, seemingly asleep. Ardeshir went up and shook his sister by the shoulder. Her neck lolled and her head fell sideways. The servants recoiled as Ardeshir took her hand. It was cold and lifeless. There was no pulse.

Anahita was dead.

Ardeshir and the servants walked back to the kitchen, shocked to the core. There was complete silence for a while.

'We must get a doctor,' said Parvati.

It was a sensible suggestion, so it was decided that Ram Singh would drive to Dr Sharma's residence and bring him back in the car. There was no telephone at Darlington Hall.

Dr Sharma arrived within half an hour. He confirmed that Anahita was dead.

'There will have to be an autopsy to confirm the cause of death,' said Dr Sharma. 'We have also got to inform the police as I am not sure that it is a natural death.'

'What do you mean?' exclaimed Ardeshir. 'What has happened to my sister?'

'I cannot say with certainty. We have to follow the proper procedure,' said Dr Sharma. 'I will write a note for the police inspector. It should be delivered to the police station immediately. Meanwhile I will remain here.' His calm, authoritative voice had an impact. Dr Sharma sat down and wrote a note for the police inspector that he handed to Ram Singh. 'Go immediately and ensure that he reads it in front of you.'

Ram Singh's departure left an awkward silence. The servants slowly dispersed and Ardeshir went up to his room to get dressed.

There was a little delay in the police's arrival. The inspector had gone to the White Palisades Hotel to investigate a petty theft. Ram Singh was directed there by the station house officer, and so he finally found the inspector at the hotel. His work having been completed, the hotel manager had offered him a cup of tea. They had joined a table where Jamshed and Avijit were finishing breakfast.

'With your permission, may we join you?' said the manager.

'Yes, certainly,' said Jamshed courteously. He introduced himself and Avijit. The inspector's face lit up and he extended his hand.

'It's a pleasure to meet you, sir. My name is Ajay Baluni. We have heard about how you solved the case of the missing widow in Bombay. I believe you are a famous detective!' said the inspector.

Avijit laughed. 'That was a rather simple case. It turns out that the widow had never been missing anyway.'

'Please tell us about it,' said the inspector.

Avijit had just started telling the story when Ram Singh walked up, holding his chauffeur's cap in his hands.

'I beg your pardon for interrupting, but I was told at the police station that I would find you here. I have a message for Inspector sahib from Dr Sharma,' said Ram Singh. He extended the note which the inspector read immediately.

'Good heavens!' he exclaimed.

Jamshed looked at him enquiringly. 'What has happened?'

'It seems like somebody has died at Darlington Hall,' said the inspector.

'Who?' said Jamshed. A worried frown had gathered on his brows.

'Her name is Anahita Bilimoria,' said the inspector reading out from the note.

'What!' exclaimed Jamshed. He got out of the chair and snatched the note from the inspector.

Avijit put a restraining hand on the inspector's arm. 'She is his wife.'

'We must all go to Darlington Hall immediately,' said the inspector. 'What is your name, driver?'

'Ram Singh, sir.'

'Go up to St Catherine's Hospital immediately and tell them to send a stretcher team to Darlington Hall. The house is right below the hospital,' said the inspector. 'We will go to Darlington Hall in my jeep.'

The driver salaamed and departed.

The inspector telephoned the police station and asked the station house officer to immediately send a team of policemen to Darlington Hall. He then got into the police jeep along with Jamshed and Avijit, and they left the hotel. They reached the house in fifteen minutes.

Agnes let them in. The inspector asked her to call everyone staying in the house including the servants to assemble in the drawing room. She left and returned soon afterwards with Ardeshir and the other servants.

'I will be questioning each one of you. You cannot leave the house until I give you permission,' said the inspector sternly.

He then walked up to Anahita's room along with Dr Sharma. Avijit and Jamshed too accompanied him. Jamshed walked into the room and let out a cry of grief. He wanted to go close to Anahita, but the inspector stopped him.

'Please do not touch the body,' said the inspector. 'Please go down and wait in the drawing room with the others.' Jamshed looked as if he was going to argue with the inspector but thought better of it. He turned and went down the stairs.

The inspector introduced Avijit to Dr Sharma. 'He is a famous detective, Doctor. Perhaps we are lucky that he is here today. Anyway, what is your first impression?' said the inspector.

'I can't say without an autopsy to confirm, but I think she may have had an overdose of sleeping powder. Apparently, she was in the habit of having them every day and may have taken too much,' said Dr Sharma.

'So, it may be an accident?' said the inspector.

'It's too early to say. The autopsy should give us more details,' said Dr Sharma with professional caution.

'Let us go and talk to the people downstairs while we wait for the medical team. Coming, gentlemen?' said the inspector.

'I will just take a look around,' said Avijit.

'Please do not touch anything,' cautioned the inspector and Avijit nodded. They walked away, leaving Avijit in Anahita's bedroom. He spent a few minutes looking around and then came down to join them in the drawing room.

'I would like to speak to each of you alone,' said the inspector. By this time, the police reinforcements had arrived and so had the medical team. The police photographer and a constable who had been trained in forensics went up to Anahita's bedroom. Dr Sharma went with them.

The inspector and Avijit, along with a police stenographer, stationed themselves in the morning room. Agnes was the first person they spoke to. After the initial, formal questions, the inspector asked her, 'What happened yesterday?' Agnes recounted the events of the morning and the heated argument between Ardeshir and Marjorie that resulted in the latter walking off to the retreat.

'What happened after that?' said the inspector.

'Well, that bitch came back in the evening and madam really let her have it,' said Agnes viciously.

'Please, no abuse. What was the argument all about?' said the inspector.

'I could not hear everything as the door was closed,' said Agnes, gesturing to the door of the room where they were sitting.

'But you did hear something,' said the inspector.

'They were having a heated argument, but we could not hear clearly. I gave them coffee, but they fell silent when I came in. Later, madam shouted out very loudly,' said Agnes with relish.

'Loud enough for you to hear?' said the inspector. 'What did she say?'

Agnes hesitated. 'I am not very sure.'

The inspector stared at her for a long moment. 'What happened afterwards?'

'Madam dragged Marjorie up the stairs to her bedroom. She was screaming that she was being drugged, but I could not fully understand what she meant,' said Agnes.

'Was madam having any sleeping powders?' said the inspector.

'Yes, they had been brought by Marjorie from the retreat,' said Agnes.

'How did she have them?' said the inspector.

'I think she used to mix them in the milk that I gave her at bedtime. I never actually saw her having them,' said Agnes.

Agnes confirmed that she had indeed taken Anahita's milk up to her room the previous evening.

'Madam was half asleep when I came in. She did not get up or talk to me, so I have no idea whether she drank the milk last night,' said Agnes.

'She did drink the milk. The glass was empty this morning,' said Avijit.

'Well, I did not notice when the door was broken and we all went in,' said Agnes.

'Did Anahita get up and lock the door when you were leaving after giving her the milk?' said Avijit.

'I don't think so, sir. She was almost asleep when I went in,' said Agnes.

'But the door was locked from inside in the morning?' said Avijit.

'Yes, sir,' said Agnes.

'That means that Anahita got up, drank the milk, and locked the door at some point during the night,' said Avijit. 'After which she died.'

They were all silent as they thought about what Avijit had said.

'Did you hear anything at night? Could something have woken her up?' said the inspector.

Agnes nodded. 'Ardeshir baba knocked over his bedside table by mistake at night. There was a very loud noise.'

'Could it have woken up Anahita?' said the inspector.

'I could not say,' said Agnes.

The inspector looked at Avijit, who nodded.

'You can leave now, but we will need you again later,' said the inspector. 'Please ask Ardeshir to come up.'

'That murdering, filthy lot at the retreat is responsible for her death, Inspector! You catch hold of them and hang them,' snarled Agnes as she was getting up from the chair.

'Please keep quiet. The law will proceed against anyone who has committed a crime,' said the inspector sternly.

Ardeshir was the next to be interviewed. After the initial questions, the inspector said, 'Why did you come to Mussoorie?'

'Agnes called me and said that my sister was unwell and that she had come under the influence of a fraud god-man,' said Ardeshir.

'Have you been in touch with Agnes earlier?' said Avijit.

'Yes, she has kept in touch with me throughout. She has looked after me since I was born as my mother died in childbirth,' said Ardeshir.

'What exactly did Agnes tell you?' said Avijit.

'Well, the whole story, I guess. She said that Marjorie had been giving her a sleeping powder and that Vishwa Jyoti was a fraud. She feared for my sister's health and felt that it was necessary for me to come to Mussoorie immediately,' said Ardeshir.

'Anything else?' said Avijit.

'No,' said Ardeshir with some hesitation and then more strongly added, 'That was all.' The rest of Ardeshir's testimony corroborated what Agnes had already told them.

'You can leave now, but you cannot leave Mussoorie until we give you permission. We may need to talk to you again,' said the inspector.

'I think we need to meet Marjorie and Vishwa Jyoti,' said the inspector. 'The others can be interviewed by the station house officer.'

Avijit agreed and they came out of the morning room. The police photographer had taken all the photographs that he wanted, and he had left to have them developed. The medical team was waiting for them. They asked permission to take the body to the mortuary. The autopsy would be performed by a police surgeon who would come from Dehradun the next day. The inspector agreed to this, so the body was removed by the stretcher team.

The forensic team had swept Anahita's room for fingerprints. These would now be tallied with each person in the house.

'We have taken the empty glass of milk. It needs to be analysed,' said the head of the forensics team.

The inspector had a few words with the servants and told them to stay in the house. He left a constable to guard the premises and then left for the retreat with Avijit. Jamshed had already left for his hotel.

12

Questions at the Retreat

The retreat looked calm and serene as the inspector and Avijit, accompanied by a police stenographer, walked up the little path. The sound of chanting was dying down as they came in. The morning discourse was getting over. They had arrived right on time. The inspector walked in and asked a retreat worker in an authoritative voice about the leaders' whereabouts. 'Where are Vishwa Jyoti and Marjorie?'

The worker pointed to the prayer hall from which the devotees were just emerging. They walked into it and went to the dais where Vishwa Jyoti was still sitting.

'Vishwa Jyotiji, namaste,' said the inspector politely.

Vishwa Jyoti got up and said, 'Namaste, what brings the police to this place of worship?'

'I need to ask you and Marjorie some questions,' said the inspector.

'About what? And who is this?' said Vishwa Jyoti.

'This is Avijit Sikdar, the famous detective,' said the inspector.

'Oh ho, so now the police need the assistance of private investigators!' said Marjorie. She had been standing quietly behind Vishwa Jyoti until then.

'Do not take offence,' said Vishwa Jyoti. 'What do you want to talk about?'

'One of your devotees is dead,' said the inspector.

'Who?' said Vishwa Jyoti.

'Anahita Bilimoria,' said the inspector.

'What! How did she die?' said Vishwa Jyoti.

'She was found dead in her bed this morning,' said the inspector. 'I need to ask you a few questions.'

'Well, if it was a natural death, you would not be asking questions,' said Vishwa Jyoti.

'I am asking the questions, Vishwa Jyotiji,' said the inspector. Vishwa Jyoti nodded; his eyes were watchful.

'How long have you known Anahita?' said the inspector.

'I first met her in Bombay. She was greatly troubled and unhappy and found a lot of solace in the retreat in Powai. Later, she wanted to come to Mussoorie so that she could meet him personally,' said Marjorie before Vishwa Jyoti could respond. 'Anahita was very unhappy about her father's death, as he was her biggest support. She was desperate to communicate with him and Vishwa Jyotiji was able to help her with that.'

If the inspector or Avijit were amused or sceptical about the seances and the summoning of dead spirits, they did not say so.

'Why did Anahita want to communicate with her father?' said the inspector.

'She was unsure of her relationship with her husband and wanted his guidance,' said Marjorie.

'Why don't you answer yourself, Vishwa Jyotiji?' asked the inspector.

'Vishwa Jyotiji does not remember what happens in the seance,' explained Marjorie.

The inspector wasn't convinced with her answer, but he let it go. 'So, what advice did she get from her father?' said the inspector.

Marjorie hesitated and looked at Vishwa Jyoti for help. But he did not say anything, so she finally said, 'He told her that her husband was a good man.'

'I see. Was she convinced?' said the inspector. He looked less than convinced himself. 'Are there any drugs used in the retreat?' said the inspector.

'Drugs? Why should we use drugs?' said Vishwa Jyoti, a look of annoyance on his face.

'Is it true that you introduced Anahita to sleeping powders?' said the inspector directly, pointing to Marjorie.

'Yes, she was not sleeping well. We have a doctor attached to the retreat and it was he who prescribed the sleeping powder,' said Marjorie.

'Why was Anahita angry with you and Vishwa Jyotiji?' said the inspector, turning to Marjorie.

'It was that woman, Agnes, who poisoned her mind!' said Marjorie.

'Why did she do that?' said the inspector.

'How do I know? Ask her,' said Marjorie.

'What happened?' said the inspector.

'After Anahita had spoken to her father, her mind was deeply unsettled. Vishwa Jyotiji told her that she should not attend another seance, as it would be harmful for the spirits who would come to talk to her. She used to come to the retreat every day, but after some time, she just stopped,' said Marjorie.

'What happened then?' said the inspector.

'Her brother appeared,' said Marjorie shortly. 'He was very insulting and rude to me.' Marjorie's face darkened as she remembered the insults that Ardeshir had heaped on her. 'He said all sorts of demeaning things and made false and baseless accusations about the retreat and about Vishwa Jyotiji.'

'What sort of things?' said the inspector.

'Well, he said that the retreat preyed on women,' said Marjorie. Her eyes were flashing and she looked very upset.

'We are a spiritual organisation, Inspector. Such accusations are totally baseless and slanderous,' said Vishwa Jyoti.

The inspector considered his next words carefully. He was about to say something and then thought better of it.

'Tell me what happened last evening,' said the inspector.

'Ardeshir's behaviour had been thoroughly obnoxious during the day. I spoke to Vishwa Jyotiji about it and, as usual, he advised me to forgive them,' said Marjorie. 'I came back last evening to try and make up with Anahita, but it did not happen. Instead, she appeared to have almost gone mad. She hurled all sorts of abuses at me and accused me of drugging her. She dragged me upstairs to her bedroom and slammed the door.'

'What happened then?' said the inspector.

'She took out the packets of the sleeping powder and flushed them down the toilet,' said Marjorie.

'Where were the packets kept?' said Avijit.

'They were kept in a wooden box on her bedside table. The box had the design of an elephant inlaid on the lid,' said Marjorie.

'And then?' said the inspector.

'She told me to get out of the house,' said Marjorie. Her voice was trembling and her hands were shaking as she spoke. 'I went down the stairs and left the house. Agnes slammed the door behind me.'

'What time did you leave the house?' said the inspector.

Marjorie considered. 'I think it may have been around seven in the evening or a little before that. I can't exactly remember.'

'You did not come back to Darlington Hall later that evening?' asked the inspector formally.

'No, there was hymn singing going on in the prayer hall. I joined the crowd and later after the session was over, I told Vishwa Jyotiji about what had happened. He consoled me and I went to sleep after dinner.'

'Where are your quarters?' said the inspector.

'There,' Marjorie said, pointing towards the administrative block. 'Vishwa Jyotiji's personal quarters are in the top two floors. I have a small room on the first floor.'

'Well, that will be enough for today. Both of you cannot leave Mussoorie unless I give you permission,' said the inspector. The Inspector and Avijit said namaste and left the retreat.

'I would love to hear your observations, Mr Sikdar,' said the inspector. 'If you permit, we will return to the police station as I have a lot of paperwork to do. I can offer you a cup of tea,' he added.

Avijit agreed, so the police driver drove down Camel's Back Road towards Picture Palace. The police station was in Kulri, on the Mall Road, just before the cinema hall. It had a narrow entrance next to a mandir. The station house officer saluted as the inspector walked in. He went to his room with Avijit following. They sat down and the inspector asked for some tea to be brought in. A young boy from a small tea shop nearby came with little glasses and a teapot. The tea was sweet and milky. Avijit sipped appreciatively while the inspector was caught up with the pending paperwork that a major case entailed. At last, he gave a sigh of relief and looked up. He closed the file that he was sifting through and smiled at Avijit.

'I am sorry I made you wait. I look forward to your views,' said the inspector.

'It's a strange case,' said Avijit reflectively. 'The victim, if she is one, was in a room locked from inside and we have three sets of people who may have had a motive for her death but no visible method of doing away with her.'

'So, you feel that she is not a victim? In other words, it was either suicide or an accident?' said the inspector.

'No, I don't necessarily feel that,' said Avijit reflectively. 'Events seem to have moved at a very rapid pace. The brother and the husband arrive, the evil influence is dramatically evicted, and Anahita dies in her bed. All in a trice! It's rather melodramatic, don't you think?' said Avijit.

'I notice that you don't exclude Jamshed from the list of suspects. Developing on that theme, perhaps he hired you, a famous detective, to get rid of his wife for some obscure reason,' said the inspector laughing.

'The reason is hardly obscure, Inspector. He stands to gain from her death. I don't exclude anyone on principle. Certainly not my friends, for they are the most likely people for whom I might have an error of judgement,' said Avijit rather formally.

'Fair enough. So, what do you really think?' said the inspector.

'Well, it is clear enough that Anahita was being drugged. I'm not sure whether we should buy the retreat version of prescribed sleeping powders to help her sleep. The question is why,' said Avijit.

'There have been some rumours about this Vishwa Jyoti. Rather unsavoury ones. We don't have any concrete evidence yet, but there are reports that he has been preying on women in more ways than one,' said the inspector. 'Most of the devotees are women and there have been quite a few wealthy women who have signed over their property to the retreat.'

'Marjorie's befriending of Anahita in Bombay and then bringing her to Mussoorie does smack of a set-up,' said Avijit.

'But the problem is that Marjorie was not present in the house that evening and Anahita's door was locked from inside. So, even if she wanted to do away with her, how did she do so?' said the inspector.

'How indeed! We do not have any information yet and as the greatest detective of them all said, it is a capital mistake to theorize before one has data,' said Avijit.

'Then there is the obvious nexus between Agnes and the brother,' said the inspector. 'Something quite serious triggered the panic telephone call that summoned him to Mussoorie.'

'In the event of Anahita's death, the heir to her considerable fortune is the next of kin, her husband and brother,' said Avijit.

'So, what you are implying is that Agnes saw or heard or found out something that could change the status quo?' said the inspector. 'And why should she be more loyal to Ardeshir than her mistress? After all, her employer was Anahita. Is it possible to take her statement at face value—that she had called Ardeshir as she thought Anahita was in trouble?'

Avijit shrugged. 'All this is in the realm of speculation. As of now, we are faced with the basic question: how did she die? If that becomes clear, it may be easier to proceed to the next question: why?'

'I just have a feeling that a lot of people are lying. I don't know for what reason. In fact, the reasons could all be different,' said the inspector.

'All right, let us list the principal players. There is Anahita herself, her brother Ardeshir, her maid Agnes, her husband Jamshed, and the people from the retreat: Marjorie and Vishwa Jyoti. What lies do you think they are telling?' said Avijit.

'Let's take the retreat. Going by rumours, Anahita may have been a target for extracting money. Hence, they drugged her. To what end, we can speculate, but they have told us a lie about the fact that they drugged her as her physical condition was far worse than mere sleeping powders would cause. Second, I get the feeling that there was some event that turned Anahita against the retreat. Maybe she got to know something about them. I don't think her behaviour changed only after her brother arrived. Something had happened earlier,' said the inspector.

'Very good,' said Avijit. 'What about the others?'

'If we take Agnes, I think she has lied about why she called Ardeshir so urgently. Something must have happened that precipitated it. I also think that she has not told us the entire truth about what she heard that evening when Anahita and Marjorie were arguing. The same goes for Ardeshir,' said the inspector.

'That is a fair summary of what we have seen so far. What about Jamshed?' said Avijit.

'You will be able to tell us more about him,' said the inspector.

Avijit told him the story about how Jamshed and Anahita had met, got engaged, and subsequently married. He had not been present at the Sheesh Mahal at the Avikanksh Palace for the engagement or the wedding as he was in England at that time, but Jamshed had told him the whole story that Avijit now retold.

'He has told me that he wanted to come to Mussoorie so that he could be close to Anahita and try to convince her to come back to him,' said Avijit.

'That sounds fair enough,' said the inspector.

'It may be, but I must caution you that I have not been in very close touch with Jamshed after his days at Oxford,' said Avijit. 'There is an obvious motive. If Anahita decides to leave him, he loses her considerable fortune. If she dies intestate before that happens, he stands to inherit 50 per cent of her fortune, with the rest going to her brother. That is a considerable amount. Perhaps he came to Mussoorie with the intention of doing away with her.'

'It sounds a little far-fetched. However, I think the point is that he should also be on our list of suspects, provided of course it is a murder,' said the inspector.

'Precisely. We must be careful to avoid speculation without data. When do you expect the results of the autopsy and the other forensic work?' said Avijit.

The inspector shrugged. 'We have no forensic capability

at Mussoorie and even the Dehradun staff is not very experienced. The autopsy will be performed tomorrow at St Catherine's Hospital. If they need to consult Delhi, it may take some time. They need to examine fingerprints as well as the analysis of the glass of milk and the body.'

Avijit got up to leave. 'Thank you very much for involving me in your work today. Let us wait and see what comes out of the forensic work. I will be at the White Palisades Hotel. I presume you want Jamshed to stay in Mussoorie?' said Avijit.

'Yes, he should not leave without our permission,' said the inspector.

'I will tell him that. Good evening, Inspector,' said Avijit.

***

'I really loved her, Avijit,' said Jamshed. The more formal salutation had long been discarded as the two men had become friends over the years.

They had walked over to the Lexton Plaza and were having a drink at the famous Hunter's Bar after Avijit had returned from his meeting with the police inspector. Import restrictions had taken their toll and now the men sipped Old Castle rum rather than single malt whisky.

'I don't doubt that,' said Avijit.

'I admit that I had several girlfriends earlier. I'm no spring chicken, but Anahita was different. She seemed so pure, so true,' said Jamshed. 'She had misunderstood my relationship with Suman. After her marriage, in which she is very happy, we have remained friends. I really value her capabilities and that is why I decided to appoint her as a manager in the company.'

'I understand,' said Avijit. He let Jamshed talk as he seemed really upset and unhappy. When he stopped talking, after a while, he spoke again. 'Did you know Anahita's father?'

'Yes. He was a doyen amongst Parsi traders and businessmen. In a sense, my business is modelled on what he did,' said Jamshed.

'Were you his rival?' said Avijit.

'Not by a long chalk! Mr Bilimoria was far ahead of me, and I was a mere youngster while he was a well-established businessman. I am a self-made man, as you know. My father died when I was quite young, though he did leave some money that paid for my education. After that, I was on my own,' said Jamshed.

'Would it have been advantageous for you if you could have merged your business with Mr Bilimoria's?' said Avijit.

'I see what you are driving at. I'm not a fool. Many people felt that my marriage with Anahita was driven by that motive,' said Jamshed.

'And was it?' said Avijit.

'No. I have searched my heart and asked myself this question again and again. But no, I really loved her,' said Jamshed, his voice breaking.

'Hmm. Well, the police are likely to ask you questions about how you felt when Anahita rejected you,' said Avijit.

'Why? Am I a suspect?' said Jamshed a bit agitatedly. 'Besides, she did not reject me. Ours was only a little misunderstanding.'

'Everyone is a suspect if a murder has been committed. As of now that has not been established,' said Avijit.

During a lull in their conversation, the manager at the Lexton Plaza walked up to their table. 'I beg your pardon for interrupting, but I wanted to offer my condolences,' he said.

It was evident that the news of Anahita's death had spread like wildfire in the small hill station.

'Thank you,' said Jamshed. He looked a little put out by the imposition but spoke politely. Despite that, the manager lingered on.

'There was a death in this hotel sixty years ago. A British lady was murdered in a locked room,' said the manager.

'What has that got to do with this?' said Avijit.

'The principal suspect was her companion, in whose favour the lady had just changed her will,' said the manager.

Avijit was suddenly interested. 'What happened then?'

'The companion was away from the hotel and, in fact, out of Mussoorie when the lady, Margaret, died,' said the manager.

'I see,' said Avijit.

'If you would pardon me, I recognized you as Avijit Sikdar, the famous detective, and I thought I would tell you the story,' said the manager.

Avijit inclined his head in acknowledgement. 'I fail to see what that story has to do with what has happened now.'

'Perhaps nothing. The companion, Miss Catherine Levitt, was involved in seances and spirituality,' said the manager.

'What happened after that?' said Jamshed, his curiosity piqued.

'Margaret's brother contested the will and he won. The companion was arrested for murder but later acquitted as there was no evidence. She returned to England afterwards. The murder was never solved,' said the manager.

There was a contemplative silence after the manager had finished speaking.

'There is obviously no link between what happened sixty years ago and now, but the press have already got hold of it. There was a reporter asking questions this afternoon. I thought I would tell you,' said the manager. '"Past events cast their shadows, and stranger things have been known to happen," was the reporter's remark after he had heard the story. Once again, my apologies for intruding,' he added and with that, the manager withdrew.

'Well, that's a very strange story!' said Jamshed.

'Strange indeed! No rational person can admit a link between an unconnected event sixty years ago and what is happening now. I suggest we forget about it,' said Avijit.

'I doubt if the press and public will let us do that,' said Jamshed presciently. 'Let's get out of this place. I think I need some fresh air. Let's have dinner somewhere else.'

They walked down to the library and decided to eat at the Glass Room. The Mall Road was full of people. A happy, chattering throng of summer visitors paraded past the open glass windows that gave the eponymous restaurant its name. Dinner over, they strolled back to the White Palisades Hotel.

13

Good News

Arnavaz Bilimoria returned from her appointment with Dr Jehangir Mistry, the renowned gynaecologist at the Khusrow Maternity Hospital, in a glow of elation. She was going to be a mother! She could hardly wait for the evening when her husband, Bahram, would return from work so that she could share the good news with him. It was the month of May in Bombay and the monsoon had not broken yet. The heat was oppressive and Arnavaz found even the act of walking up the few steps to the front door of the Bilimoria mansion on Malabar Hill tiring. She fell into an exhausted sleep but woke up feeling refreshed in the early evening.

She bathed and changed and was waiting for Bahram when he walked in at seven. He came in and accepted a glass of lemonade from his wife with a sigh of satisfaction.

'I went to meet Dr Mistry today,' said Arnavaz.

'Dr Mistry? The…' said Bahram.

'Yes, the gynaecologist,' said Arnavaz excitedly. 'I'm pregnant!'

Bahram got to his feet with a wide smile on his face. He went towards his wife and took her in his arms. 'Is everything all right? When is the baby due?' he asked.

'Everything is fine, though I get tired easily in this heat,' said Arnavaz.

'Oh! Well, we can't go to England anyway this year as war is likely to break out sometime soon and there are already restrictions on travel,' said Bahram.

'What about your office there?' said Arnavaz.

'Hopkins will have to manage as best as he can,' said Bahram with a shrug. 'In any case, trade will become a problem if, or I should say when, war breaks out.'

It was May 1939, and the drums of war were already sounding over Europe. Bahram Bilimoria ran an extensive global trading business with offices in London, Bombay, and Hong Kong. He was in the habit of spending the summer in London with his wife. This year, that programme would have to be forgone.

'Shall we go to Kashmir instead? Going abroad is ruled out,' said Bahram.

'No, I can't face the journey. It's too long,' said Arnavaz plaintively.

'Well then, the easiest hill station to get to is Mussoorie. We will take a direct train to Dehradun and now that there is a motorable road, we can get almost all the way up by car,' said Bahram. 'It's a beautiful place and the season is very lively. We can easily stay for two months. The weather will do you a world of good, my dear.'

The Bilimorias left for Mussoorie by the end of May. It was a long train journey, and they were quite exhausted by the time they reached their destination. Bahram had decided to stay the night in Dehradun rather than going up to Mussoorie immediately. It was a good decision, as the train was late and Arnavaz was thoroughly exhausted by the time they arrived. Dr Mistry had not been too pleased with their decision to travel to Mussoorie as Arnavaz, for all her good spirits, had a weak constitution but had given his reluctant approval after seeing her eager face and hearing Bahram's calm and logical arguments. They stayed the night at the railway retiring room at Dehradun station with a good dinner being provided by the railway restaurant. The next day, they set off in a taxi. The battered Austin had seen better days, but it navigated the twisting mountain road quite well. They reached the final motorable point fairly soon, after which Arnavaz went up in a *dandi* while Bahram followed on a rather broken-down chestnut horse. They reached the Lexton Plaza Hotel at noon.

'*Bonjour, madame et monsieur. Bienvenue à Mussoorie. Votre chambre est prête pour vous,*' said Maurice, the Swiss manager of the Lexton Plaza as the Bilimorias walked in.

Bahram replied politely in French. '*Merci beaucoup. Madame est très fatiguée après le voyage et nous aimerions aller immédiatement dans notre chamber.*'

'Of course, Mr Bilimoria. Ashok Singh is the butler attached exclusively to your room. He will show you to your room and will be always available for your help,' said Maurice with a bow.

Ashok was a short, clean-shaven, good-looking man. His face was indeterminate. He may have been a local, or a

Nepali, or indeed from anywhere in north India. Like many people from the hills, it was difficult to estimate his age. He was not a teenager, but he was not very old either. Dressed in the hotel uniform of a black suit with a bow tie, he looked neat and presentable. Unexpectedly, he bowed and touched Bahram and Arnavaz's feet. He took Bahram's briefcase from him and Arnavaz's purse and spoke in a soft, educated manner in English. 'Please follow me. Your luggage will have already reached your room,' he said.

Ashok led them up a flight of steps to the main building of the hotel and then still further to the wing facing the Himalayas. Their suite was on the first floor in the middle of the wing. He opened the door and ushered them in. Arnavaz immediately exclaimed at the view visible from the large windows at the opposite end of the sitting room. It had been a cloudy morning but had cleared up by now. The window opened towards the north and the view of the snow-capped mountains was spectacular. She looked out of the window as Bahram joined her. There was a drop to a narrow parapet and the road below. The sitting room was furnished in an English cottage style with chintz sofas and a coffee table. The polished wooden floor was covered with an oriental carpet. The room was quite well lit, though the only window opened towards the north. Bahram glanced up and saw that the source of natural light was a skylight in the sloping ceiling.

Ashok opened the door leading to the bedroom and stood aside to let the Bilimorias go through. There was a brass four-poster bed in the middle of the room. A desk stood near the window overlooking the mountains and there was an attached bathroom.

'Very modern fittings, I must say! I didn't expect a flush toilet in the hills,' said Bahram, impressed.

'Thank you, sir. The whole hotel has been modernized and renovated recently,' said Ashok.

'How did you learn to speak such good English?' said Bahram.

'My father put me in an English school when I was a child, sir,' said Ashok.

'Really? How could he afford that? What did he do?' said Bahram.

'He was a waiter and then a butler in this very hotel,' said Ashok.

'I see. That makes it even more strange,' said Bahram.

'You see, sir, he came into some money when I was ten years old,' said Ashok.

'Still. It is very difficult for an Indian boy from a poor background to get into such a school and that too so many years ago,' said Bahram.

'There was an English burra sahib who helped him, sir,' said Ashok.

'I see. Well, we will have a bath and change and then come down for lunch,' said Bahram.

Ashok bowed and left the room.

The Bilimorias soon settled into a comfortable routine at the Lexton Plaza. The hotel was luxurious and expensive and apart from them, most of the other guests were either Indian royalty or foreigners.

'Would you like to visit some of the scenic places in Mussoorie?' said Ashok one morning. He was serving them breakfast in their suite. It had been a few days since they had come up to Mussoorie and Arnavaz was feeling rested and energized.

'Yes! I think that's a good idea,' said Arnavaz excitedly. 'Where should we go?'

'How about the Company Gardens?' said Ashok. 'The flowers will be in bloom now. I can arrange for a rickshaw for madam and sir to ride.'

Very soon, the Bilimorias were bowling along on the flat road to the Company Gardens. Ashok accompanied the group, half running to keep pace with the rickshaw-wallahs. He was dressed in casual clothes today, having left his uniform behind. The hotel had provided a picnic lunch, the weather was perfect, and it looked like a wonderful day.

They set up their picnic on a small flat ground on a hillside covered with grass. The gardens were beautiful, ablaze with hydrangea, rhododendrons, and a host of spring flowers. The air had a drowsy feel and soon Arnavaz found herself falling into a light sleep. Bahram was walking around while Ashok stayed with Arnavaz.

'Arnavaz, look what I found! It's so beautiful! Come over here,' exclaimed Bahram. Arnavaz woke up with a start as she heard her husband's voice calling her from a distance. She stumbled as she got up suddenly and her foot slipped. She fell forward and rolled off the little flat area where the picnic had been set up.

Quick as a flash, Ashok lunged forward and grabbed her hand as she was about to roll down the hill. It was over in an instant. Ashok found his footing and gently pulled Arnavaz back from the precipice. She lay there panting. He gave her water to drink and called out to Mr Bilimoria who came running.

'What happened?' said Bahram. His voice cracked with concern as he saw his wife lying on the cloth spread out for the picnic.

'I slipped when I heard you calling, Bahram. If Ashok had not caught my hand, I would have been at the bottom of the hill,' said Arnavaz in a shaking voice.

Bahram looked over the edge of the hill and shuddered. It had been a narrow escape. He went up to Ashok and shook his hand. 'We are very thankful to you.'

'It was nothing, sahib, only my duty,' said Ashok.

'It does appear that you have been sent to look after us,' said Bahram. He looked at Ashok fondly and patted him on the shoulder. They left the Company Gardens soon afterwards.

***

'Maurice, I want to discuss something with you,' said Bahram.

'Come into my office, sir. We can talk there,' said the hotel manager.

Their stay at the Lexton Plaza was coming to an end. The monsoon had started, and the clouds lent an eerie touch to the atmosphere.

'We have had a wonderful time at the hotel,' began Bahram.

'Thank you, sir,' said Maurice.

Coffee had been brought in and Bahram was in a relaxed mood. The hotel was also less crowded as the season was almost over.

'This is a very historic building, isn't it?' said Bahram.

'Yes, the hotel opened about forty years ago. We have had a lot of famous visitors including writers like Rudyard Kipling and the Nehrus,' said Maurice.

'It is a lovely hotel and you and your team are to be complimented on how well you have maintained it,' said Bahram.

'Merci beaucoup, monsieur,' said Maurice.

'Now, coming to the reason why I wanted to talk to you. We have been extremely impressed by Ashok Singh. He is a highly intelligent and resourceful man and has an excellent command over English. I would like to offer him a job as our butler in Bombay,' said Bahram.

'I see. Have you talked to him? These Paharis are often not happy to go to the plains,' said Maurice.

'I have talked to him, and he has agreed to go to Bombay with us. However, I will take him only with your consent,' said Bahram.

Maurice considered. Finally, he spoke. 'It is your decision, of course. However, you are really taking on a person whom you know nothing about. Are you sure about this?'

'Yes. I hire people all the time. This is just one more. So, is it okay with you?' said Bahram.

'Yes, sir. It is okay. I believe you are leaving tomorrow. It has been a great pleasure having you and madam with us. We look forward to welcoming you at the hotel again soon,' said Maurice as Bahram rose to take his leave.

The Bilimorias left the next day for Bombay with Ashok Singh. Maurice and Mrs Gomes, the hotel housekeeper, saw them off.

'Well, he's gone,' said Maurice.

'Yes,' said Mrs Gomes.

They had walked into Maurice's office after seeing off the Bilimorias.

'Should we have warned them?' said Maurice.

'No,' said Mrs Gomes decisively.

'It does not seem right,' said Maurice.

'Well, we know that Ashok is a crook, but we have never been able to prove it. If we had, we would have dismissed him a long time ago,' said Mrs Gomes.

Over the years, there had been a series of robberies at the Lexton Plaza. The amounts were generally small and many of the guests had not even noticed or reported their loss. Maurice had investigated and, in some cases, the needle of suspicion had pointed towards Ashok. They had confronted him with it, but he had denied it completely and there the matter rested.

'Yes, that's true,' said Maurice.

'Good riddance is what I say,' said Mrs Gomes robustly.

Ashok established himself very quickly as the major-domo in the Bilimoria mansion in Bombay. He was a great support to Arnavaz as her pregnancy progressed and was at hand when the baby, Anahita, was born. A new housekeeper also joined the staff at that time. Her name was Agnes De Mello. Ashok soon took her under his wing.

14

Investigations

'Heiress Murdered'

'Mysterious Death in a Locked Room'

'Godman Implicated'

'Seances to Summon the Spirits of the Dead'

The headlines in the morning papers were nothing short of sensational. Jamshed and Avijit were having breakfast at the White Palisades Hotel as they read the papers in silence.

'It seems that the *Sentinel* is the paper whose reporter met the manager of the Lexton Plaza. Just see this article,' said Avijit. He handed over the paper to Jamshed, who read it for a while and burst out laughing despite his grief over the recent turn of events.

It is a well-known fact that spirits of dead people are amongst us. Margaret Maynard-Liddell, the British lady who was murdered in 1909, must be a happy woman today. Her unavenged death has found a parallel in the demise of Anahita Bilimoria. Her spirit is guiding us today to find the murderer. Was Anahita Bilimoria a reincarnation of Margaret? Inspector Ajay Baluni of the Mussoorie Police said that there was a lot to learn from past events. Does that mean that the spirits have spoken to him?

'Inspector Baluni must be really laughing at the way that the reporter has twisted his words!' said Jamshed.

'I hope he's only laughing,' said Avijit dryly.

The article went on. It was full of inanities, innuendoes, and plain speculation. However, all the newspapers were unanimous in declaring Vishwa Jyoti's retreat to be a den of vice. There was much pleasurable speculation about went on in there.

The *Daily Voice* said rather portentously:

It is not in the interests of civil society to allow such fake retreats and godmen to survive, nay thrive. We have heard the most reprehensible tales of the goings-on in the retreat which are not suitable for printing in a newspaper that will be read by families. We must unite to stamp out this menace. All this mumbo jumbo about spirits and seances is not good for our society.

Thus, the newspapers were divided on the influence of the spirits—whether they existed at all and, if they did, whether they were evil or beneficent. All in all, it was a heady mix, and coming as it did smack in the middle of the tourist season, it created a stir, the likes of which had rarely been experienced in the hill station.

'And this is only the beginning. It will get worse,' said Avijit as he put down the newspapers with a sigh.

***

The police released the body from the morgue after the autopsy had been performed, and it was brought to Darlington Hall in a hearse. It was placed in the drawing room in a coffin awaiting the funeral. Some of Anahita's friends who were still in Mussoorie came to pay their respects, as did Jamshed and Avijit.

'She seemed quite cheerful that day when we met her at the White Palisades Hotel,' said Sharon. 'I wonder what happened after that.' There was a hint of a malicious gleam in her eye. Perhaps a twinge of envy for the privileged heiress. 'There does not seem to be anybody from the retreat here.' She had introduced herself to Ardeshir and was standing with him in the morning room along with her husband.

'Marjorie did come, but I sent her away with a flea in her ear,' said Ardeshir with some satisfaction.

'I see. You, of course, as the brother and heir apparent are in a privileged position,' said Sharon.

'I think the retreat was an evil influence on my sister and it is best they stay away,' said Ardeshir a bit pompously.

'Oh, indeed,' said Sharon as Ardeshir left her to go back to the drawing room.

Anahita was to be laid to rest in the Parsi cemetery on Camel's Back Road. Most of the guests had left by late afternoon. It was a sombre group that walked behind the hearse the short distance to the cemetery. The burial was soon over, and the mourners walked back to Darlington Hall. A Parsi priest had come from Delhi for the rituals, as there were virtually no Parsis left in Mussoorie or Dehradun. He took his leave after the burial as he wanted to hurry back to Delhi.

Inspector Baluni was waiting for them at Darlington Hall. He took Avijit aside and said, 'The results of the autopsy and forensics have come in.'

'What are the findings?' said Avijit.

'Anahita died as a result of an overdose of Seconal,' said the inspector.

'The sleeping powder?' said Avijit.

'Yes. It could have been the sleeping powder that had been prescribed to her by the retreat doctor,' said the inspector. 'We need to verify the prescription.'

'I see,' said Avijit contemplatively. 'So, it could have been accidental.'

'It may have been. Seconal has a slightly bitter taste, and she would've had to have rather a lot of it,' said the inspector.

'She used to mix it in her nightly glass of milk,' said Avijit.

'The curious thing is that the remnants of milk in the glass kept on her bedside table show no traces of Seconal,' said the inspector.

'How did she have it then? That remains the most intriguing question,' said Avijit.

The inspector nodded.

'What is the estimated time of death?' said Avijit.

'The doctor has been cautious on that front. He says after midnight and before four in the morning, so that is a pretty big range. She could have died any time during the night,' said the inspector.

'What about fingerprints?' said Avijit.

'The glass of milk has Agnes's fingerprints overlaid with Anahita's. Other than that, there are prints of all the household members as they all walked into Anahita's room when they broke the door down,' said the inspector.

'So, we are really none the wiser,' mused Avijit. 'She died in a room locked and bolted from inside and we have no idea how the sleeping powder was ingested.'

The two looked at each other. Finally, the inspector said, 'Let's go up to her room again. Perhaps we will find some inspiration.'

Avijit agreed so they walked up the stairs.

The entrance to her room was in the middle of an open corridor that ran around the house on the inside, overlooking the hall. The door had still not been repaired by order of the police and a yellow tape was stuck across the open doorway to prevent anyone from trespassing. The inspector peeled it aside and both stepped into the room. There was a thin film of dust covering the tables, as the room had not been dusted since the day Anahita was found dead. Everything had been left as before including the unmade bed.

On the right of the door, as they entered, there was a dresser. The room key was lying in a small porcelain bowl kept on top of the dresser. There was a photograph of Anahita's father in a silver frame and another of Anahita and Jamshed, taken in London. Adjacent to the dresser and forming an L was a closet. On the far wall to the right was the door to the bathroom. In the front, as they entered, was an area set up as a small sitting room with a large window behind it. There were prints of classical paintings on the walls in ornate frames whose gilt was beginning to wear off. It was evident that the decor was impersonal, as could be expected in a house which the owners did not use to live in themselves but gave on rent.

'All the windows are barred. You can open them, but nobody can get in,' said the inspector as they looked around the room.

On the left of the room with the headboard against the wall of the connecting room a brass four-poster bed was located. It had a window on the far side that had a view of the Himalayas. There were side tables on both sides with reading lamps.

The inspector and Avijit walked to the bathroom door and opened it. The bathroom had been modernized and tiled, but the original clawfoot bathtub had been retained. There was a vanity cabinet above which was a mirror that opened with a hinge. The inspector opened it. It had the usual complement of toothpaste, skin cream, shampoos, and so on.

They went back to the bedroom and opened the closet. It had feminine clothes, both saris and western wear, and a range of shoes below. Anahita was a well-dressed, stylish woman and her closet confirmed the fact.

They went out of the room and into the corridor. On the right were three bedrooms overlooking the mountains. The one nearest was occupied by Ardeshir. On the left was one bedroom which was mostly used as an additional sitting area, as it had a window opening on the hill side with little natural light. There was a storeroom adjacent to it. On the far side, opposite Anahita's room, were two bathrooms opening out on the corridor. There was really nothing of note, so they went back to Anahita's room.

On an impulse, the inspector picked up the wooden box lying on Anahita's bedside table. He opened it to see that it contained a few small paper packets as dispensed by a chemist. Surprised, he opened one of them. There was a white powder inside. He gingerly tasted it. It was slightly bitter.

'Just look at this!' said the inspector. 'It could be Seconal.'

Avijit came up and tasted the powder. 'Yes, it could be.'

'This needs to be analysed. I'm surprised that the forensic team missed it,' said the inspector. He put a few packets in his pocket.

'I wonder,' said Avijit. His eyes were gleaming and there was a suppressed excitement in his voice.

15

The Will

Jamshed and Ardeshir were sitting in the drawing room in silence when the inspector and Avijit came downstairs. Agnes came in and asked them whether they would have tea and they all acquiesced. A pall of gloom had settled thickly over the room.

'Well, Inspector, what conclusion has the police reached?' said Ardeshir a bit mockingly.

'Our investigations are ongoing,' said the inspector impassively.

'I can't understand why you don't arrest the retreat crowd. It's obvious that they have done it,' said Ardeshir.

'I'm afraid the police need to have some proof before we make a move,' said the inspector.

Agnes came in with the tea tray. She had just poured out the tea and handed the cups over when the doorbell rang. She got up and returned soon with a pink telegram, which she handed over to Ardeshir. Many telegraphic condolences had been received after Anahita's death and Ardeshir assumed that it was another one. His expression changed as he read the message and then he read it aloud.

ARRIVING MUSSOORIE TOMORROW STOP IMPORTANT DEVELOPMENT RE ANAHITA WILL STOP TARAPOREWALA

'I wonder what it can be,' said Ardeshir almost casually, as if it did not really concern him.

The inspector and Avijit looked at each other. 'We should be going,' said Avijit as they got up to leave.

'I will also come with you,' said Jamshed.

They took their leave and drove off in the inspector's jeep. They dropped Jamshed at the White Palisades and then Avijit and the inspector drove to the police station on the inspector's invitation. They settled down in the inspector's room with glasses of tea. The inspector called in Constable Gupta, who came in, saluted, and stood at attention.

'Were you part of the team that went to Darlington Hall?' said the inspector.

'Yes, sir,' said the constable.

'Did you find any drugs or powder wrapped in packets like these?' said the inspector.

The constable thought about it. 'I don't think so, sir, otherwise it would have been in the report.'

'Could they have been kept in the wooden box on Anahita's bedside table and you did not examine it all?' said the inspector.

'I didn't personally look at the wooden box, as I was searching the bathroom, sir,' said the constable. 'We did a very thorough job, sir, and it is very unlikely that we missed something like this. If there were no packets in the box, the report would not have mentioned anything, as we were reporting only what we had found, not what we did not,' said the constable with impeccable logic.

The inspector sighed. 'You are right, Gupta. Dismissed,' said the inspector. 'Oh, before you go, please send these packets for analysis.'

The constable saluted and left the room.

The inspector pulled out the file of the records of the forensic team when they had examined Darlington Hall and went through it carefully.

'As Gupta says, there is no mention of any such packets. They would have certainly reported it if they had found something,' said the inspector. 'There is also no specific mention of the objects that they have examined. Hence, no proof of if they actually looked at the box or not.' The inspector was looking at the file as he spoke, so he missed the gleam in Avijit's eyes. 'Let me check on Marjorie's statement. I think she had said something about the packets.'

The inspector pulled out another file and read Marjorie's signed statement. 'It's very clear. She says that Anahita had taken the packets and flushed them down the toilet. I suppose she flushed them all,' he said with a hint of a question in his voice.

'We found too many packets in the box for them to have been left there by accident after Anahita threw them away,' said Avijit.

'Then was Marjorie telling a deliberate lie? If so, it's quite damaging,' said the inspector.

'Also, inexplicable. If the packets were there in the first place, it would have been easier to conclude that it was an accidental death,' said Avijit.

'There is also the fact that the glass of milk did not have any traces of Seconal in it,' said the inspector.

'That ties in with what Marjorie said. If there were no packets of the powder left in the house, Anahita could not have put some in her milk,' said Avijit.

'If so, there must have been some other way for her to have ingested the powder,' said the inspector. 'We have been over this ground before. We are now going around in circles.'

Avijit got up to take his leave. 'I think we need some fresh thinking on this,' he said as they shook hands.

'Yes. I'm also getting a lot of pressure from above about the retreat. It seems that public opinion has completely turned against Vishwa Jyoti, but we do not have any grounds to act on,' said the inspector.

Avijit strolled back towards the White Palisades Hotel. On the way, he stopped to buy newspapers from Sethi Book Depot. A cursory glance at the headlines brought out a sigh of resignation.

'Police Lax As Usual' was the *Sentinel*'s headline. 'Despite more than enough news and information about Vishwa Jyoti and his evil activities, the police are doing nothing. Is there pressure from the godman's powerful friends that has stayed the course of justice? The chief minister needs to answer for this,' said the article. There was much more, and a similar tone was echoed by most of the other newspapers also.

'The press is having a field day,' said Jamshed as Avijit joined him in the hotel restaurant for lunch.

'There is a message for you, sir,' said a waiter gesturing to Jamshed. Ram Singh came up with an envelope that he handed over to Jamshed.

Jamshed's eyebrows rose as he read the note. 'You can tell Mr Ardeshir that we will both be there,' he said to Ram Singh, who nodded and left.

'Dr Taraporewala wants us to be present when he comes tomorrow. Apparently, another telegram has arrived at Darlington Hall after he tried to contact me in Bombay and learnt that I was in Mussoorie. He said that he is expected by late morning, so he has asked me to come over to Darlington Hall at 12 noon,' said Jamshed. 'As you saw, I have agreed that both of us will be there.'

'This should be interesting. Normally, money is the strongest motive behind any crime. Until now, I had assumed that Anahita's money would pass onto you and Ardeshir, but I wonder what is in store,' mused Avijit.

***

Jamshed and Avijit were greeted by Agnes as they walked into Darlington Hall at noon the next day. Mussoorie weather was at its exhilarating best and both men had discarded heavy woollens in favour of a light cardigan worn over casual trousers. The crowds on the Mall Road were building up as the morning progressed, but Camel's Back Road was quiet. It was a sunny day, and the snow-capped peaks were visible in their full glory.

'Ardeshir baba will join you shortly. Would you like some tea or coffee?' said Agnes as she showed them into the sunlit morning room.

Ardeshir walked into the room. He shook hands with both men and said, 'Dr Taraporewala has arrived and will be with us soon.' There was a suppressed excitement in his voice. They had barely seated themselves when Agnes came into the room again.

'Marjorie has arrived,' said Agnes in a controlled voice.

'What! Why is *she* here? Tell her that we cannot see her and that she is not welcome here,' said Ardeshir in a loud voice.

'She told me that Dr Taraporewala had asked her to come,' said Agnes.

There was a stunned silence. Agnes turned around and came back, with Marjorie following her. She did not greet anyone but took her place quietly on a sofa by herself.

Dr Taraporewala came in carrying a slim leather briefcase. He apologized for being a little late and introduced himself. 'I regret that I was unable to come for Anahita's funeral. I had some urgent work to attend to that made my leaving Bombay impossible. Jamshed, I am truly sorry about what has happened. It is a great tragedy.' He shook hands with Jamshed and put his arm around his shoulder. He then sat down, put on his reading glasses, and opened his briefcase.

'Ardeshir, I am sorry for your loss as well,' said Dr Taraporewala. 'Anahita was a good sister. She always took your side, even when I advised her against it.'

Ardeshir nodded. He said nothing. There was an expectant silence in the room.

'Just two days ago, I received a letter from Marjorie,' said Dr Taraporewala, gesturing towards her.

'What! How did she have the cheek to write to you!' exclaimed Ardeshir.

Dr Taraporewala held up his hand. 'I was understandably surprised to receive her letter, coming as it did so soon after Anahita's death.'

'What did she say?' said Ardeshir impatiently.

'I will read the letter aloud,' said Dr Taraporewala.

'Dear sir, I wish to inform you that we are in possession of Anahita Bilimoria's will. It was signed on 7 May 1973 at Mussoorie. I am enclosing a copy. Kindly advise us of the next steps,' read Dr Taraporewala. 'The letter was signed by Marjorie Richards and a copy of the will was enclosed. Briefly, without getting into details, it leaves the whole of Anahita's fortune to Vishwa Jyoti's establishment. The will was witnessed by a doctor and a lawyer who are both based in Mussoorie. I have been appointed as the executor.'

A complete silence greeted Dr Taraporewala's words. Finally, Marjorie spoke. 'We are deeply grateful to Anahita for thinking of the retreat. She was a great devotee of Vishwa Jyotiji and it is right that she has endowed the retreat with her wealth. The original will is kept in the retreat safe.'

'This is a complete fraud!' said Ardeshir heatedly, jumping to his feet and shaking his fist at Marjorie.

'May I leave now?' said Marjorie.

Dr Taraporewala nodded. 'I will be in touch with you separately to fulfil the formalities,' he said. 'Even though it is not strictly required, it will be best to apply for a probate of the will from the court since the estate is substantial and it has been left to someone who is *not* next of kin.'

'Thank you, Dr Taraporewala. We will await your arrival at the retreat,' said Marjorie, getting up to leave the room.

Jamshed and Avijit had been silent throughout. After Marjorie's departure, Avijit spoke, 'It appears that the will may not have been registered, as I don't think Anahita went to the court to do so. Does that present a problem?'

'No, a will does not have to be registered,' said Dr Taraporewala. 'Further, Anahita was free to leave the estate to whomever she wanted. The estate was self-acquired by Mr Bilimoria, not inherited by him, and hence he could leave it freely to whomever he liked. It is not ancestral property in its strict legal meaning. I'm afraid that, technically, Anahita was within her rights to leave the estate to the retreat.'

'Can the will be contested?' said Ardeshir.

Dr Taraporewala looked at him consideringly. 'Are you intending to do that?'

'Why not? My sister was being taken for a ride by these charlatans. She was being drugged and was not in her senses. Is that not reason enough?' said Ardeshir. 'I am bloody well convinced they have done away with her, and I will be damned if I let them get her money too.'

'Her death is already a police matter,' said Dr Taraporewala.

'Yes, and I hope they get a move on. Well, do I have the grounds for challenging the will?' said Ardeshir.

'You can challenge a will on several grounds. 'Undue influence, is possibly the one that could apply. You will need to consult a lawyer though,' said Dr Taraporewala.

'That's exactly what I am going to do,' said Ardeshir. There was silence after he spoke.

'Well, my work here is done. It is better that I stay at a hotel rather than here,' said Dr Taraporewala. 'I still need to visit the retreat and take custody of the will.'

'You could stay at the White Palisades Hotel, where we are staying, Doctor,' said Avijit. 'We are not allowed to leave Mussoorie until the court gives us permission.

'Yes, that is a good idea. I will first walk across to the retreat and then come to the hotel. Agnes, I will send someone to pick up my bags. They are lying in the room upstairs,' said Dr Taraporewala.

The three left Darlington Hall together. Avijit pointed out the direction of the retreat to Dr Taraporewala, who walked towards it while the other two went back to the White Palisades Hotel.

16

An Arrest

Public speculation and interest in the Mussoorie mystery refused to die down. It was partly fuelled by the press who came up with increasingly sensational and bizarre theories.

'Magician Questioned'. The *Sentinel* report bordered on the ludicrous as usual. Most of it was pure speculation, or worse, fabrication.

The police today confirmed that they had questioned Mr Basil Culpepper, a touring magician. He had been present at Miss Maynard-Liddell's birthday celebrations on 27 July. How he managed to enter the party is a mystery as none of the people involved knew him. Mr Culpepper claims that he had received a telepathic cry of help from Miss Maynard-Liddell and had gone there on her invitation. A little bird tells us that Mr Culpepper had wanted to read Miss

Levitt's mind at the party, but she had left the room hurriedly when he approached! Clearly the spirit world had foreseen the events to come. Poor Miss Maynard-Liddell! Her spirit cries out for succour. Is there no spiritualist who can talk to her and ask her how she died?

The actual police questioning had been far more mundane. The magician had regretfully conceded that he had not been allowed to read Miss Levitt's mind, whatever that meant. In any case, all this speculation did nothing to advance the case further.

Captain Willoughby met Dr Williams again. 'I believe Miss Maynard-Liddell was in the habit of consuming sodium bicarbonate,' said the captain.

Dr Williams nodded. 'She suffered from dyspepsia. I had prescribed it for her.'

'Is it possible that a dose of prussic acid had been mixed with the sodium bicarbonate that was found in the bottle next to her bed?' said the captain.

'Very unlikely. If someone did it a few days ago, it would have surely killed her earlier. Prussic acid is a deadly poison,' said Dr Williams. 'If it had been done on the night before she died, the poison should have still been in the bottle. We know that the analysis results did not show anything.'

'What other possibility can there be?' said the captain.

'It cannot be that she ingested the poison before going to bed. Prussic acid is extremely fast-acting and death occurs very soon. So, she must have had it at night after going to her room,' said Dr Williams. 'If so, who gave it to her and how?'

'Miss Levitt is the obvious suspect. Mr Carrington told me in confidence that he is facing a lot of pressure due to mounting public opinion and that she may be arrested. In that event, could there be any possible way that she could have perpetrated the crime? We need to carry conviction with the judge,' said the captain. 'I trust that you will keep this conversation confidential.'

'Indeed. I fail to see how she could have done it. Apart from anything else, she was in Lucknow on the day of the crime and had been there for quite a while,' said Dr Williams.

The two men sat in silence for a while. Clearly, the mystery did not allow for an easy or obvious solution.

Miss Catherine Levitt was arrested in mid-November. Public outcry against her had refused to die down. The ASP had been summoned by the superintendent of police in Dehradun.

'Sit down, Carrington,' said Arthur Green, the SP for Dehradun district.

'Thank you, sir,' said the ASP. He saluted and sat down at the edge of his chair. He had a fair idea of what was coming.

'Have you made any progress on the Maynard-Liddell case?' said the SP.

'No, sir. We are at a dead end,' said the ASP frankly.

'You know very well that the obvious suspect is Miss Levitt. Why don't you go out and arrest her?' said the SP.

'There is no evidence against her,' said the ASP uncomfortably.

'I will be frank. The public is incensed by what they see as police incompetence. The world at large is convinced that she is the murderer and that the police are dragging their feet,' said the SP.

'We will lose the case in court, sir,' said the ASP.

'Let us cross that bridge when we come to it. Right now, I need everyone from the lieutenant governor downwards off my back,' barked the SP. The meeting was clearly over, so the ASP got up, saluted, and withdrew.

Miss Catherine Levitt was arrested for the murder of Margaret Maynard-Liddell in mid-November. As the *Sentinel* reported,

Final Seance

It is a matter of satisfaction that the police have finally done their duty. It is a matter of great public importance that crime should not go unpunished. The arrest of Miss Levitt for the murder of her benefactor is the first step in this process. We are certain that the courts will hold the same view.

Rather unfortunately for that pompous piece of reportage, the courts did not uphold the view that Miss Levitt was guilty. The case came up for trial in the district court, where it was swiftly demolished for lack of evidence. It was referred to the Allahabad High Court, but the verdict was the same. There was no convincing evidence against Miss Levitt, and she was set free.

Around the time when Miss Levitt was arrested, the poet Orson Dankworth disappeared. There were some rumours that he had contracted cholera due to his association with some of the women of the lower classes, as they were euphemistically known in Dehradun, and that his body had been hastily cremated. However, he was never seen again.

Immediately after the high court verdict in her favour, Miss Levitt applied for a probate of Miss Maynard-Liddell's will that had been made in her favour by cutting out the family. The probate was contested by the Maynard-Liddell family, which was represented by Colin Maynard-Liddell. This also created a sensation, and all the intriguing and salacious aspects of the case got a new lease of life. The district court judgement went in favour of Colin Maynard-Liddell. Miss Levitt's application was rejected on the grounds of undue influence, especially due to crystal-ball gazing and other means of clouding the victim's judgement. The Allahabad High Court also upheld the judgement. Miss Margaret Maynard-Liddell's estate passed on to her family.

Miss Levitt returned to England. Was she innocent or guilty? The mystery was never solved.

17

A Brainwave

'Did you know that hydrangeas have different colours, either pink or blue, depending on whether the soil is acidic or alkaline, Jamshed?' said Avijit.

The two friends were enjoying their walk around Lal Tibba and had stopped to admire the hydrangeas growing in one of the houses just below the circular walk. Jamshed nodded. He was aware of Avijit's eclectic mind. Quite different from the maxims of the Great Detective, who always maintained that 'the skilful workman is very careful indeed as to what he takes into his brain-attic'.

'Just look at the orderly perfection of the garden below. The hydrangeas are arranged in perfect colour coordination and pruned to perfection. And look at that bed of petunias! The colours match perfectly with the antirrhinums at the back. The owner must be an artist or a musician or perhaps a professor of mathematics,' said Avijit.

Jamshed smiled. 'Like yourself.'

'Oh, unlike me. I don't have the patience to run a house anymore,' said Avijit with a tinge of sadness. The death of his wife was still fresh in his mind and Jamshed fell silent.

The walk was shaded by deodar and silver oak trees. Here and there a rhododendron tree grew. With its gnarled branches and spiky leaves, the flowers made a brilliant display. Crimson splashes of colour amidst the shade of the old trees. On the northern side, near Arthur's Lodge, the snow view was spectacular, and the two friends sat on the concrete border of the road to admire the everlasting snows. They wandered into the cemetery and read the inscription on the base of an old tree that had been planted by the then Duke of Edinburgh in 1871.

Avijit was perfectly dressed as usual in a tailored brown tweed suit with brown brogues and a tweed cap. His gold-rimmed glasses added to the professorial look. Jamshed was more casual with his jeans and leather jacket. They had decided to take a walk the day after Anahita's will had been discussed. Dr Taraporewala had taken the original will in his custody as the executor and had left for Bombay. The retreat represented by Marjorie had formally communicated their intention of proceeding to obtain a probate for Anahita's will in the Dehradun District and Sessions Court. He had sent a note to Ardeshir informing him about the retreat's decision and had told Jamshed and Avijit as well. He had then left for Bombay in the morning and the two friends had decided to take a walk after seeing him off at the Picture Palace taxi stand.

They made their leisurely way around the circular walk back to Char Dukan, where they stopped to savour the ginger lemon tea that was one of the specialities of all four of the stalls. Later, they strolled through Landour Bazaar, stopping at the Ganesh Café opposite the Craggy Hill Estate to sample the masala dosas for which the café was justly famous.

'This coffee is simply the best in the world,' said Avijit with a contented sigh. They were feeling replete and were sipping Ganesh Café's excellent south Indian filter coffee at the end of the meal. It was almost three o'clock by the time they finished, and they started the walk down to Picture Palace past the clock tower.

As they were passing by the police station at Kulri, a constable stopped them. 'The inspector would like a word with you, sir. He saw you walking past.'

'Yes, certainly,' said Avijit, and the two friends made their way to the police station. The inspector ushered them into his room.

'Should I leave?' said Jamshed.

'No, please stay. This will only take a minute. I wanted to tell you that we have received a complaint about the retreat from a woman who claims to have been molested by Vishwa Jyoti. It is a very serious complaint, and I was just getting my team ready to go to the retreat. We have a search warrant and an arrest warrant for Marjorie and Vishwa Jyoti,' said the inspector.

'Whew! That is news indeed,' said Avijit.

'Hopefully, we will find something incriminating,' said the inspector. 'I must leave now, and I would request both of you to say nothing about this matter.'

'Yes, indeed. Good luck, Inspector,' said Avijit.

'I suspect that public pressure was becoming too much. The police had to act,' said Jamshed. They were walking down the Mall Road towards the White Palisades Hotel and stopped to see the posters at Minerva Cinema. *Love Story* had just been released in India and so had the Amitabh Bachchan blockbuster, *Zanjeer*. 'I haven't seen a movie in ages. Somehow business has been so hectic.'

'Yes, you are a busy man. Perhaps it's best for you to remain busy at this time,' said Avijit. 'One of the things that puzzles me is why did Anahita suddenly change her opinion about the retreat? It must have something to do with what she saw or heard there.'

'Hopefully, the police will find something,' said Jamshed.

'What is your opinion on the case so far, Avijit?' he asked later that evening. They were sitting in the hotel bar and there had been no word from the inspector.

'There are several puzzling things about the case,' said Avijit. 'Let me list them down as follows.' He proceeded to write on a table napkin.

- How was the narcotic administered? We know that Anahita had a cup of coffee in the evening, then dinner, followed by a glass of milk at bedtime. We also know that there were no traces of the narcotic in the glass of milk. The coffee cups and the dinner plates had been washed. It was an Indian-style dinner with everyone helping themselves from the same serving dishes, so it's unlikely that the narcotic could be given only to her. That leaves the coffee. It is possible that the narcotic was given to her in the coffee. It would explain the fact that she was feeling unusually sleepy that evening. But it does not tie in with the time of death, which is after midnight, while the coffee was had around 6.30 in the evening.

- There was a loud crash at night. We have been told that it was due to Ardeshir having knocked over his bedside table. Is there anything significant about this?

- Agnes said that when she left Anahita's room after leaving the milk on her bedside table, her room was unlocked. Yet, it was found locked from the inside in the morning and the key was on the dresser. It was also bolted. A part of the bolt was later found on the floor after the door was broken open in the morning. So did Anahita get up at night, ingest the narcotic herself and lock the door before going back to bed?

There was a long silence after Avijit finished speaking. Just when Jamshed was about to suggest dinner, Avijit sprang up. His eyes were gleaming. 'It is so obvious! I am a complete imbecile. We must go to Darlington Hall immediately!'

'Now?' said Jamshed. 'It's nine o'clock!'

Avijit looked a little crestfallen. 'Yes. I suppose we can't just barge into the house.'

'Can it wait? If it's very urgent, we will go right away,' said Jamshed.

'No. It can wait,' said Avijit. His eyes were still gleaming, and his hand shook a little as he sipped his whisky.

***

'Bogus Godman Arrested', screamed the headlines of the *Sentinel* the next day. There was a picture of Vishwa Jyoti and Marjorie with handcuffs as they were being led to a police jeep while a crowd of devotees watched in shocked silence. 'This newspaper has always maintained that Vishwa Jyoti is bogus. We are glad that the police have finally seen it fit to arrest him. The activities at the retreat are in not in keeping with civilized society. We have heard horrific tales of rape and embezzlement that are too graphic to be printed in a family newspaper.'

'The way they have suddenly tailed off! It's clear that they know nothing apart from the fact that these two have been arrested,' said Jamshed with a guffaw.

The inspector walked up to the table where the two friends were having breakfast. 'Good morning. Would you like to come to Darlington Hall with me? We can talk on the way.'

Avijit and Jamshed accepted with alacrity, as that was anyway what they had wanted to do, and they were soon on their way in the inspector's jeep.

'We raided the retreat yesterday,' said the inspector.

'Really? What did you find?' said Avijit.

'Nothing. The retreat was as clean as a whistle. They have had enough time to get rid of any evidence. We have taken their bank papers and accounts into custody. They are very rich indeed! Their modus operandi seems to be to prey on wealthy, susceptible women, but there is really no proof of coercion,' said the inspector.

'What about the woman who complained about them?' said Jamshed.

'Again, it's what she says. She has no witnesses and so far, none of the retreat staff has said anything incriminating. We have taken Vishwa Jyoti and Marjorie into custody. Let's hope someone talks,' said the inspector. 'Right now, they are in police custody, and I will have to produce them before a magistrate by tomorrow. I am going to Darlington Hall with the hope that Ardeshir or Agnes can tell us something incriminating.'

***

Avijit and the inspector sat down in the morning room. The inspector asked Agnes to remain there. He told them about the arrests at the retreat, which they had already read about in the newspaper. He also told them about the complaint of molestation that the police had received. Ardeshir congratulated the inspector and said, 'I had always known that Vishwa Jyoti was bogus. I am glad someone complained.'

'Do you know anything that could corroborate any of this?' said the inspector. 'Think carefully.'

Agnes and Ardeshir looked at each other. Finally, Agnes spoke. 'Madam said that Vishwa Jyoti is nothing but a rapist and that the retreat is a den of vice.'

'Really? Have both of you heard this? And why did you not tell me this when I questioned you after Anahita's death?' said the inspector sternly.

'No, sir, only I heard it as I was close to the door. Madam was shouting at Marjorie,' said Agnes. 'I did not speak then, as it did not look nice.'

'Did she say how she knew that this Vishwa Jyoti was a rapist. Think carefully before you speak,' said the inspector.

'No, Inspector, she did not say why or how she knew about that,' said Agnes reluctantly.

'Is there anything else that you can tell me that you have not so far,' said the inspector.

'No, sir. I don't know anything else,' said Agnes and Ardeshir nodded. The inspector instructed the police stenographer to record the statement and get Agnes to sign.

'I would like to meet the maid who cleans the rooms,' said Avijit after the inspector had finished. The inspector looked at him with a puzzled expression but gestured to Agnes, saying, 'Please ask her to come in.'

Agnes looked undecided but turned around and came back with a Pahari woman who looked very scared. She was dressed in a *ghaghra* with a full-sleeved blouse in typical Pahari fashion.

'There is nothing to be afraid of,' reassured the inspector in Garhwali. 'We just want to ask you a few questions.'

'We need to go upstairs. Are any of the rooms locked?' said Avijit.

'No, they have just been cleaned and they are all open. Madam's room's door is not repaired yet. The police have allowed us to clean it,' said Agnes.

She started accompanying them as they walked towards the stairs, but the inspector stopped her. 'You stay here please.'

They first walked into Anahita's room on Avijit's direction. 'Please describe what you saw on the morning that she died. You were also with all of them when the servants came up, weren't you?' said Avijit in Hindi, which the woman understood fairly well.

'Yes, I also came up, but Agnes didi told me to go and clean up Ardeshir sahib's room,' said the woman.

'I see. So, you did not enter the room at all?' said the inspector.

'No, sir. The driver and the gardener were attempting to break down madam's door when I went into Ardeshir sahib's room,' said the woman.

'What did you see in Ardeshir's room?' said the inspector.

'The bed was unmade, and the bedside table had fallen down. There was broken glass and water lying on the floor. I went outside to get a broom and a mop from the kitchen to clean the floor,' said the woman.

'Had madam's door been broken down by then?' said Avijit.

'Yes, sir, it broke just when I came out of Ardeshir sahib's room. There was a loud crash,' said the woman.

'What did you do?' said Avijit.

'I stopped and stayed to watch,' said the woman.

'I see. What happened then?' said Avijit.

'They all went in. Agnes was the last to go in. She saw me standing outside and told me to get on with my work, so I went downstairs to fetch the cleaning things. I did not see anything, Inspector sahib,' said the woman.

'What happened afterwards?' said Avijit.

'I came down and picked up the cleaning things. Meanwhile, they had all come down and I heard them sending the driver to get a doctor,' said the woman.

'What did you do after that?' said Avijit.

'I cleaned up Ardeshir sahib's room,' said the woman.

'Can you show us Ardeshir's room?' said the inspector and they all walked into the adjoining room.

The inspector opened the door. It was a small room with just enough space for a bed and a small dressing table with a cupboard next to it. A window opened out to the mountains on the far side of the bed. The bed had bedside tables on both sides and the headboard was against the wall between Anahita's room and the room where they were standing. The table near the window had a ceramic bedside lamp, while the

table near the door had only a tray with a glass jug and a glass
for drinking water.

'Which table had fallen over?' said Avijit.

'This one, sir,' said the woman, pointing to the one near
the door. 'There was a bedside lamp on it, just like the other
one and a tray with a jug and a glass. They had all smashed.
It made a very loud sound at night and even I woke up. You
see, I sleep on a mattress in the kitchen,' said the woman.

Avijit gestured quietly to the inspector, who
understanding his signal, took the woman outside and went
to the next room.

Avijit walked over to the bedside table. It was in a corner.
It was an old-fashioned table with a drawer and was made
of solid wood. He tried to pick it up and found it to be really
heavy. He tried to overturn it, but it required quite a lot of
effort. It could only fall forward as there was no space on
the other three sides. It was certainly not the kind of table
that could overturn by somebody stumbling into it at night.
Besides, anyone getting out of the bed would not find the
table in their path.

Avijit came out of the room and joined the inspector
and the cleaning woman in the next room. 'Did you go
back to sleep after you heard the loud crash in the night?'
said Avijit.

'Not immediately, sir, as I felt disturbed,' said the woman.

'Did you hear or see anything else?' said Avijit.

The woman hesitated. 'I think I heard footsteps, sir, but
I can't be sure.'

'When?' said Avijit.

'Later, when I was just getting back to sleep,' said the
woman.

'Thank you. If there is something that you remember later, please make sure that you tell us,' said the inspector. They all walked down the stairs.

'Both you and Agnes are required to stay on in Mussoorie for a while. The retreat people have been taken into remand and we may need more investigation. However, the matter of Anahita's death is different, and our investigation is still underway,' said the inspector to Ardeshir as he took his leave.

'I really wonder whether Agnes is telling the truth or is this just a way of bolstering the case against the retreat,' said the inspector as they were driving back in his jeep.

'Does it really count as evidence? A good lawyer would make mincemeat of it,' said Avijit.

'You are right. It's Agnes's word against the retreat's. Also, the fact that she did not speak earlier is very damaging,' said the inspector. 'Anyway, I need to present them to the magistrate tomorrow. Let's see what he says.'

'I would like to go out of Mussoorie for a while,' said Avijit. 'I hope I have your permission.'

The inspector looked at him questioningly. 'I presume you will eventually tell us what you are thinking,' he said with a smile.

Avijit's eyes were gleaming. 'You can count on it, Inspector.'

18

A Writer Investigates

Rudyard Kipling Esq.
Bateman's,
Burwash,
East Sussex, England

4 May 1910

Dear Mr Kipling,

I am delighted to hear that your trip to India has been finalized. I know that you will be very busy with your lectures in Bombay and Delhi, but it will be a great pleasure for me if you could find the time to visit Dehradun and Mussoorie.

The Mussoorie murder has reached a remarkably interesting stage as Miss Levitt has been acquitted by the district court. It will be a pleasure to discuss it with you in person.

Yours sincerely,
Charles Harewood

***

Charles Harewood Esq.
Ashridge
Rajpur Road
Dehradun

29 May 1910

Dear Charles,

I will certainly come to Dehradun and Mussoorie. Will let you know the details soon.

In haste,
Rudyard Kipling

***

It was the end of June by the time Rudyard Kipling finished with his lecture tour and, with a sigh of relief, took the night train from Delhi to Dehradun. Charles Harewood was there to receive him at the station and Kipling greeted his younger friend with much affection. They were soon ensconced in Harewood's Bungalow.

'I must say you have a very pretty establishment here, Harewood,' said Kipling.

'You must have missed India,' said Harewood. They were having lunch in the dining room with an old-style punkah flapping overhead.

'More than I can tell you,' said Kipling. 'It's in my blood.'

By mutual consent, the discussion about the Mussoorie murder was postponed till after dinner and the two friends were comfortably seated in the gol kamra. The brandy decanter had been plied liberally when finally Kipling spoke about it.

'So, I hear that Miss Levitt has been acquitted,' said Kipling.

'Yes. There was clearly no evidence against her, and she was in Lucknow in any case when the murder was committed, so the judge had no hesitation in acquitting her. The Crown has taken the matter to the high court, but there really is no likelihood of her being declared guilty,' said Harewood.

'Then who else could be the murderer and how was the crime committed?' said Kipling musingly.

'That's a real puzzle. Nobody else stands to gain from the crime and there is really no way that anyone could have got into the room. Maybe it was "murder by suggestion". There's a lot of this occult stuff floating around,' said Harewood.

Kipling gave a sceptical snort. 'Nonsense, my dear chap! This is the twentieth century, and we are all men of science. There's no such thing.'

'Margaret's brother is in Dehradun, and he has agreed to meet us tomorrow,' said Harewood. 'Maybe you will get some more information from him.'

Harewood and Kipling met Colin Maynard-Liddell at the Dehradun Officers Club the next morning. As they settled down on comfortable wicker work chairs on the wide veranda, it started to rain—gently at first and then more steadily. The waiter brought their orders of gin and tonic along with the peanut masala and cheese balls that the club was famous for.

'Club food in India is so nostalgic. I think it will never change,' said Kipling presciently. 'Thank you for meeting me, Mr Maynard-Liddell.'

'May I know what your interest in my sister's unfortunate demise is, sir?' said Colin, a shade stiffly.

Kipling's eyes narrowed. 'Why, the same as yours surely! To bring the murderer to justice.'

'I know you are a famous man, sir, but I fail to see what you can achieve,' said Colin.

'Perhaps nothing, but there is no harm in trying,' said Kipling easily.

'The police are already on the job, but they have failed miserably in my opinion, as that evil woman has been acquitted,' said Colin heatedly.

'So, you believe that she was the murderer? Although she was not in Mussoorie on the day of the murder?' said Kipling.

'Of course, she is the murderer! She must have hypnotized my poor sister,' said Colin.

'Why did you come to India?' said Kipling.

'Surely that is obvious! My sister's will was entirely misguided and it had to be contested,' said Colin.

'So, you knew about the will?' said Kipling

'What does that have to do with this? Have you come here to pry into my affairs?' said Colin sneeringly. His face was red with anger, and he seemed to have difficulty in controlling himself.

'I don't know why you are getting agitated, Maynard-Liddell. Please calm down,' said Harewood soothingly.

'Well, I am in no mood to be subjected to an inquisition by you, Mr Nosey Parker Kipling,' said Colin. 'Good day, gentlemen.' Colin pushed back his chair abruptly and stalked off the veranda.

'Well, he's quite a firebrand,' said Kipling. There was an amused and thoughtful expression on his face. 'He does seem to have arrived in India very quickly indeed.'

'I apologize for his behaviour,' said Harewood.

'Nothing to do with you, dear boy. When should we go to Mussoorie?' said Kipling.

'We will go up tomorrow morning. I have booked rooms for us at the Lexton Plaza, and I've spoken to the police. They will be happy to meet you,' said Harewood. 'We also have a meeting with the ASP, Mr Carrington, this afternoon.'

***

The meeting with the ASP was at his office in the main police station.

'I am a great fan of your writing, Mr Kipling,' said Mr Carrington. 'How come you have become interested in our little murder mystery?'

'Hardly a "little" murder mystery, sir. It has become quite a talking point in England, too,' said Kipling.

'I'm sure we haven't come out looking very well,' said the ASP ruefully.

'Well, it is a complex matter. Do you have any views on what may have happened other than the obvious one of Miss Levitt having accomplished the murder by some occult means?' said Kipling with a smile.

'No. We have wracked our brains, but there is nothing we can think of,' said the ASP frankly.

Kipling nodded. 'I trust you have no objection to my poking around a little.'

'Well, sir, the case has already been taken up by the high court. So, even if any evidence is unearthed now, unless it is noticeably clear and specific, it will be difficult to change the path the case is taking,' said the ASP matter-of-factly.

'I appreciate your frankness. It is very unlikely that I can come up with something concrete. If I do, I will share it with you immediately,' said Kipling.

'Inspector Vijay Rathore will meet you at the Kulri Police Station in Mussoorie. He is a highly intelligent officer and has been involved in the case from the very beginning,' said the ASP.

The ascent to Mussoorie took most of the next day. They reached the Lexton Plaza only in the afternoon and were greeted by Mr Schmidt, the hotel manager.

'Welcome to the Lexton Plaza, Mr Kipling. It's a great pleasure to have you and Mr Harewood here with us,' said Schmidt. 'The suite which was occupied by Miss Maynard-Liddell has been shut after the unfortunate incident. There are many people who have reported seeing her ghost floating down the corridor.'

'Thank you. It looks like you have a full house,' said Kipling as he looked around the crowded lobby.

'Yes, sir, people have been intrigued by the murder,' said Schmidt. There was a smile of satisfaction on his face and he all but rubbed his pudgy hands together in satisfaction.

'I have allotted you the suite next to the one that was occupied by the unfortunate lady. It is identical in all respects. Mr Harewood's room is in the main wing,' said Schmidt. 'Rajesh is your room butler. He will show you to your room and will be available for your exclusive use at all times. He was the butler for Miss Maynard-Liddell also.'

Rajesh bowed and gestured for the two gentlemen to follow him. Kipling spoke to Rajesh in fluent Hindustani after Harewood had left for his room. 'Where are you from? You don't look like a Garhwali.'

'My family is from Himachal, sahib. We come from a village near Kashmir,' said Rajesh.

'That explains it. What happened here?' said Kipling. It was an abrupt question.

'Nothing, sahib,' said Rajesh. He had an unblinking gaze that was steadily focused on Kipling, who found it slightly unnerving.

'What do you mean nothing? The memsahib died!' said Kipling.

'Yes, sahib,' said Rajesh.

'You are the butler for these rooms. You must know how someone can enter the room. Well?' said Kipling. 'Do you have a master key?'

'Yes, sahib, but the room was bolted from the inside. It could not be opened by a key only,' said Rajesh. It was evident from the speed of the response that he had been questioned along the same lines by the police. He paused as the door opened a crack. A little boy poked his head in and then came in silently. He clung to Rajesh's legs. The resemblance was unmistakeable.

'Your son?' said Kipling.

'Yes, sahib. His mother died a few years ago. After that I am all that Ashok has,' said Rajesh apologetically.

'Don't worry. I am not angry,' said Kipling with a smile.

They met with Inspector Vijay Rathore the next day at the Kulri Police Station. Over cups of milky tea, the inspector briefed them about the case.

'There is little to add, sir,' said the inspector. 'We are at a standstill as ASP sahib has already told you.'

'What happened to Orson Dankworth?' said Kipling.

'He disappeared,' said the inspector.

'Wasn't that suspicious, coming so soon after Miss Maynard-Liddell's death?' said Kipling.

'Yes, sir, it was suspicious, but we could not find any link to Miss Maynard-Liddell's murder. Mr Dankworth was a bit of a strange character,' said the inspector.

'Very strange indeed! The papers are saying that he was into drugs and all sorts of other things,' said Harewood.

'Suppose for a moment that he was the murderer or had been hired by someone to commit the murder. Later, when he became too greedy, he was disposed of,' said Kipling.

The inspector looked polite but sceptical. He did not say anything.

Kipling laughed. 'Perhaps a writer's imagination can add intrigue to anything.'

The two friends walked back down the Mall Road to the Lexton Plaza Hotel.

'I don't think we have anything concrete here, Harewood. We may as well go back tomorrow,' said Kipling. Harewood nodded.

They parted at the main building, agreeing to meet for a drink before dinner at the bar. Kipling was surprised to see the little boy waiting for him as he walked up to his suite.

'How are you, son?' said Kipling in Hindi. He opened the door to his room and beckoned to the boy to follow him inside. Kipling gave him a chocolate that the hotel had left for him in a crystal bowl on the coffee table. Ashok accepted it shyly and carefully opened the wrapper.

'Do you go to school? How old are you?' said Kipling.

Ashok said that he was ten years old and that he was going to go to the big English school from next year.

'That's very nice,' said Kipling. He was quite surprised to hear that but did not say so. It was most unusual for an Indian butler's son to gain admission to an English school.

'What do you like to do?' said Kipling.

'I like to climb,' said Ashok proudly.

'Very good. There are so many mountains in Mussoorie for you to climb,' said Kipling.

'Not mountains. I like to climb ropes,' said the boy unexpectedly.

'I see,' said Kipling laughing. 'Now run along. I must dress for dinner.'

***

'I'm glad I came to Mussoorie, even though we've not found anything new,' said Kipling as he met Harewood that evening.

'I will write to you in case anything new comes up,' said Harewood.

They left Mussoorie the next day and Kipling returned to England soon afterwards.

19

Poona Findings

Avijit left Mussoorie that evening. He had been lucky to get an air-conditioned berth on the Mussoorie Express leaving that night for Delhi. He had a shower in the train bathroom and went straight to the Delhi airport, where he had lunch in a restaurant. Afterwards, while waiting for his flight, Avijit placed a trunk call to Dr Taraporewala in Bombay and obtained the information that he needed and his permission to proceed as per the plan that he had outlined. He had telephoned Indian Airlines from Mussoorie and had reserved a seat for himself to Bombay by IC 405 that left in the afternoon, so he had plenty of time. He drove straight from Santa Cruz Airport in Bombay to Dadar and took a taxi to Poona. He checked into the Green Emerald Hotel in Koregaon Park late in the night.

The address which he sought was close by in the leafy environs of Koregaon Park. He had asked the hotel for a car for the day, and the short drive took barely ten minutes. The house was a large bungalow built on two stories with a garden in front. There was a white painted wooden gate leading to a driveway. On the brick door post were two brass name plates. Ardeshir Bilimoria lived on the first floor.

Avijit asked the driver to park outside. He pushed the wooden gate open and walked in, his footsteps crunching on the gravel drive. The first floor was accessed by a door that was open. Once inside, there was a staircase leading up and another door that led to the ground floor. Avijit climbed up the broad staircase and rang the bell. After a wait, the door was opened a crack by a young manservant.

'What do you want?' said the servant. He spoke in Marathi that Avijit knew slightly.

'I have come from Dr Taraporewala's office,' said Avijit in Hindi.

'Sahib is not at home,' said the servant in Bombay Hindi. Avijit was wearing a black suit and carrying a briefcase. He looked like a lawyer.

'May I come in? I have come all the way from Bombay,' said Avijit.

The manservant opened the door and stood aside to let Avijit in. He walked into the drawing room on the right. It was a large, sunlit room with a broad balcony on two sides. The servant asked him to sit down and went inside to fetch a glass of water. Avijit looked around the room. On a sideboard, there was a picture of a woman with a new-born baby with a man standing beside them. The woman was Agnes. He quickly took out a small camera and took a picture of the picture.

The servant came and gave Avijit a glass of water that he drank gratefully. It was a warm day.

'Sahib is not here,' said the servant again. He sounded worried.

'How long has he been gone?' said Avijit.

'He has been gone for almost two weeks now and apart from a postcard from Agnes madam, there is no news,' said the servant.

'Did he leave suddenly?' said Avijit.

'Yes, there was a phone call from Agnes madam. I picked up the call and the operator said she was calling from Mussoorie,' said the servant.

'There is some bad news,' said Avijit. The servant's face changed. He looked frightened.

'Anahita is dead,' said Avijit.

The manservant did not react. 'Don't you know Anahita?' said Avijit.

'I don't know, sir. Agnes madam may have mentioned her name, but I don't remember,' said the servant. He appeared to be telling the truth.

'Anahita Bilimoria was your sahib's sister. It is in connection with her will that Dr Taraporewala has sent me here. I am a lawyer. This is my card,' said Avijit authoritatively. He handed over a card with a fictitious name to the servant, who looked at it uncomprehendingly.

'Has anything happened to sahib?' said the servant.

'I do not know,' said Avijit with a shrug. 'Dr Taraporewala wanted the passport and other important papers for your sahib urgently. Do you know where the papers are kept?' He spoke almost hectoringly, and the servant recoiled.

'There is a briefcase,' said the servant hesitatingly.

'Well go and get it! Shall I call Dr Taraporewala?' said Avijit in a threatening voice. He got up and walked to the telephone.

'Wait, I will get the briefcase,' said the servant. He returned a few minutes later with a brown leather briefcase. It was unlocked and held quite a few papers. There was a passport in the name of Ardeshir Bilimoria that gave the name of his parents as Bahram and Arnavaz Bilimoria. There was a birth certificate issued by the Bombay municipality in the same names. Sandwiched between the papers was a small leather-bound notebook. He flicked through it and saw the writing. It looked like Hindi, but he could not read it. Distracting the servant's attention, he expertly palmed the notebook. He was about to close the briefcase when he saw an envelope right at the bottom. It was open and he took the paper out.

'I need to take the passport with me,' said Avijit.

'No, sahib, I will lose my job,' said the servant. He was almost crying.

'Well then, I will need to take a photograph of some of these papers. The police will come and take the papers anyway. If they arrest you for obstructing the law, too bad for you,' said Avijit sternly.

The servant fell at his feet but would not budge. Finally, Avijit took out his camera and took photos of some of the documents. He gave the briefcase back to the servant, who took it back inside.

'I am not feeling well,' said Avijit. 'Is there a chemist shop nearby where I can buy some medicine?'

'Yes, sir, we always get our medicines from A One Medical Store,' said the servant. He sounded relieved now that Avijit had stopped threatening him.

'Do you have the telephone number and the address?' said Avijit.

'There should be some old bills lying around, sahib. I will get them,' said the servant. He came back with a few bills. The second one was a chemist's bill from A One Medical Store. The name of the patient was Ardeshir Bilimoria, and the date was the day before Ardeshir had left for Mussoorie.

'May I keep this? It will make it easier for me to find the shop,' said Avijit.

'I was going to throw away the papers anyway, sahib. You can keep it,' said the servant. 'I hope I have done nothing wrong.'

'No, you have done nothing wrong,' said Avijit as he got up to leave.

On an impulse, he asked. 'Are you alone in the house?'

'No, sir, Ashok baba is there. He has been with the family for a very long time, but he's very unwell. Would you like to meet him? He can't walk much, and the servant quarters are at the back, so you will have to go there,' said the servant.

Avijit hesitated but finally said, 'No, I don't think that will be necessary.'

His next stop was at the Koregaon Police Station. He sent in his card and after a while the inspector called him in.

'Inspector Baluni called from Mussoorie. He told me about your visit. How can I help you?' said Inspector Ajit Damle.

Avijit spoke at some length. He gave the inspector a brief rundown on the case and the reason for his visit to Poona.

'I have heard about you, sir,' said the inspector. 'It is a pleasure to meet you. What do you want from us?'

Avijit explained what he wanted. The inspector made detailed notes and promised to do what was required.

'Please wait for my call before doing anything,' said Avijit. He got up, shook hands, and left the police station. He went back to the hotel. He called Indian Airlines and booked a flight from Bombay to Delhi the next day. He was back in Mussoorie the following day. Inspector Baluni arrived at the hotel that evening. He looked crestfallen and gratefully accepted the cup of tea that Jamshed offered him in the lounge.

'What happened, Inspector?' said Avijit.

'As expected, the court refused to extend Vishwa Jyoti and Marjorie's remand. The judge said that there was no solid evidence against them,' said the inspector.

'Yes, that was likely to happen,' said Avijit.

'They have filed for probate of Anahita's will and Ardeshir has filed a case contesting the will in the same court. So, we are in for some exciting times,' said the inspector.

'The press will have a field day,' said Jamshed.

'How was your trip?' said the inspector. Avijit looked hesitant, so the inspector temporized. 'No need for you to tell me if you don't want to. I assume the trip was in connection with this case.'

'Yes, it was. I do have some important information that I will share soon. I have also spoken to Inspector Damle and he has promised to follow through with some work I have requested him to do when I call him,' said Avijit.

'Well! That certainly sounds enigmatic. Is there anything I can do to help the process?' said the inspector.

'Not really. As of now, we wait and watch,' said Avijit.

The next few days passed by peacefully apart from the sensational headlines that were a great source of mirth for all three of them.

'Bogus Godman and Moll Marjorie Want to Collar the Loot', screamed the *Sentinel* headline. It was accompanied by a cartoon of a lascivious godman and his moll, standing amidst a shower of notes with money bags strewn around them.

The court may have let off Vishwa Jyoti, but we know better. It is only a matter of time before the modus operandi of this fake godman stands exposed. He has been preying on gullible women who have signed off their wealth to him. All the mumbo jumbo about spirits and seances is just a façade to dupe the vulnerable. We have heard that he uses drugs too. While at this stage, there is no update from the police about the murder of Anahita Bilimoria, it is evident that the will and the murder are linked. Inspector Baluni has said that the police are still investigating.

'You know if this goes on for some more time, even I will start believing that Vishwa Jyoti is the murderer,' said Jamshed with a laugh.

The inspector had given permission for the two of them to leave Mussoorie, but they had decided to stay on. He had also allowed Ardeshir and Agnes to leave, but they stayed on as well. Ardeshir had walked across to the White Palisades Hotel and met them to communicate his plans.

'I intend to stay here for the time being, Mr Sikdar,' said Ardeshir.

'I see,' said Avijit noncommittally.

'I need to attend to the hearings on Anahita's will,' said Ardeshir.

'Yes,' said Avijit.

Puzzled by Avijit's cold responses, he tried another tack. 'It's a pity that the court has let Vishwa Jyoti and that bitch off. I hope they find some new evidence.'

'I'm sure the police are working hard on the case. I'm afraid I don't really have any knowledge of what they are doing,' said Avijit. 'Yes, it's a pity they were let off.'

'Absolutely! I'm so glad you agree with me. Is there any fresh evidence against them?' said Ardeshir eagerly.

'Not that I know of,' said Avijit. 'How is the will probate case coming along?'

'We have entered our written statement,' said Ardeshir. 'We have a very strong lawyer, so I think we are on solid ground.'

'Well, I wish you luck,' said Avijit.

***

The probate case lasted for a month in the Dehradun District and Sessions Court. The retreat admitted that they had been conducting seances to summon the spirits of the dead and that Anahita had participated in them.

'She was a lonely woman after her father died and her husband turned out to be unfaithful,' said Marjorie.

There was a furore after this statement. The press descended on the White Palisades Hotel and cornered Jamshed. Next day's papers carried the story. 'Husband Denies Guilt', said the *Sentinel* in rather more temperate language than it was accustomed to. The reporter had been favourably impressed by Jamshed and the tone of the article was conciliatory.

The retreat has come up with yet another canard, maligning Anahita Bilimoria's husband, Jamshed Contractor. This reporter met Jamshed, who flatly denied that he had been unfaithful to his wife.
'It is true that we had a misunderstanding, but it was not serious. I decided to come to Mussoorie to try and

persuade her to come back to me. The fact that I am still here in Mussoorie is proof enough of my devotion and desire to seek justice for her,' said Jamshed.

We understand that Jamshed's friend, Mr Avijit Sikdar, is a famous detective and that he is actively assisting the police. This fact has been confirmed by Inspector Ajay Baluni.

This paper has all along maintained that the retreat is the most likely suspect. Their leaders had inveigled Anahita into writing a will in the retreat's favour and now they are hurling accusations all over. The police and the government need to act on this.

Brother Alleges Undue Influence

Ardeshir Bilimoria alleged in court today that the retreat had exerted undue influence over his sister Anahita. 'Right from the time that she had been contacted by Marjorie in Bombay she had come under their influence. Then these seances to summon the spirit of our father! This is all mumbo jumbo. She was being drugged!'

Ardeshir's testimony had created a sensation in the court. The retreat's lawyer had vigorously objected saying that the sleeping powders were prescribed by a doctor. His vehemence was a bit diluted when he admitted that the doctor was a long-term follower of Vishwa Jyoti who lived in the retreat. The next day was even more sensational. When Ardeshir resumed his testimony, he basically accused the retreat of murder.

Brother Accuses Retreat of Murder in Open Court

We feel for the righteous indignation that a brother experiences when his sister has suffered such a terrible fate. The District and Sessions Court at Dehradun was witness to unprecedented scenes as Ardeshir Bilimoria accused the retreat, specifically Marjorie and Vishwa Jyoti, of murdering his sister. There was an uproar, with many of the people present asking for their immediate arrest. The judge had to have the court cleared. He then admonished the witness saying that this case was only about the probate of Anahita's will.

The fact remains that public feeling is running extremely high. Inspector Baluni when contacted by this paper said that he had nothing to add and that investigations were ongoing in the matter of Anahita's death. This lackadaisical attitude is a matter of grave concern. We understand that the retreat people have been let off as there is no evidence, but sometimes the will of the people must prevail.

The *Sentinel* ended on a triumphal but rather misguided note and provoked a snort of disdain from Avijit. 'I sometimes wonder what it takes to become a reporter. A nose for sensationalism and to be devoid of logical thought seem to be prerequisites,' said Avijit.

20

Court Proceedings

'I think I need to get back to the real world,' said Jamshed.

It had been over a month since they came up to Mussoorie. The court proceedings were winding down and the judge was scheduled to pronounce judgement in the coming week.

'Have patience, my friend. We are almost at the end of our stay here,' said Avijit.

'Well, you obviously know something that I don't,' grumbled Jamshed.

The two friends were on a walk towards the observatory on Benog. It was a long way from their hotel but they had persevered, taking only a short break for some tea at a dhaba near the Jesus and Mary Convent. They were now on the slopes of Benog, having crossed Hathipao and Clouds End on the way. The path was covered with pine needles and was very slippery, so both had taken the help of oak walking sticks to help them navigate better. It was also quite hot, being the month of June, so they were in shirt sleeves and wearing dark glasses to protect themselves from the intense glare of the sun. When they finally reached the summit of Benog, it was a bit anticlimactic. There was a small temple that seemed to be deserted and the ruins of a British era house. The fireplace in one of the rooms was still intact, but the roof had fallen in. It was not as interesting as had been made out, so the two soon started the descent. It was a long walk back to the Mussoorie Library and to the Jayant Restaurant that was famous for its delicious fried fish.

'Have you come to a final conclusion about who killed Anahita?' said Jamshed.

'I have, but I don't have any proof yet,' said Avijit.

'How will you obtain that?' said Jamshed.

'It is surprising how many points of similarity there are between Anahita's murder and the one in 1909,' said Avijit. He seemed to be pursuing his own train of thought. 'This fish is delicious! I think it is Himalayan trout.'

Jamshed was familiar with the way his friend's thought processes worked, so he did not interrupt.

'First, the basic idea of a murder in a locked room. Then, the mumbo jumbo of the seances and summoning the spirits of the dead. Then a will being executed in favour of the companion or in this case the retreat. The will is also being contested by the brother. All similar!' exclaimed Avijit.

'So, who was the murderer is the 1909 case?' said Jamshed.

'It was never solved! So, we don't know who the murderer was. Perhaps we will get a clue to that murderer when we solve this one,' said Avijit.

'Isn't that a bit fanciful?' said Jamshed with a hint of scepticism.

'You never know the workings of the universe. Stranger things have been known to happen,' said Avijit sententiously. Jamshed was never very sure about whether his friend was being serious or not. The two friends strolled back to the White Palisades Hotel after lunch. Inspector Baluni joined them for evening tea. He looked disheartened.

'Cheer up, Inspector, there are worse things in life than an unsolved crime,' said Avijit. His puckish mood seemed to be unabated, and the inspector looked less than pleased. He accepted a cup of tea with a rueful smile.

'It may be for you, sir. For us, it's a professional black mark,' said the inspector.

'There is hope yet. The darkest hour of the night heralds the dawn,' said Avijit. The inspector looked at Jamshed, who simply shrugged his shoulders.

'You may smile at the babbling of a lunatic, but sometimes the wisest are the ones God has touched,' added Avijit.

The inspector decided to change the topic. 'The district judge is expected to pronounce judgement in the case of Anahita's will today.'

'That is pretty fast, isn't it?' said Jamshed.

'I think the size of the inheritance is very large. There is also a lot of public interest and there has been pressure from the government. Anahita was a very rich woman and Dr Taraporewala is a very influential man,' said the inspector. 'It's now been over a month anyway.' He turned to Avijit and said, 'On a serious note, sir, are you anywhere close to finding a solution to Anahita's death? The reason why I am asking is that there have been calls that the Uttar Pradesh police has mishandled the case and that it should be handed over to the CBI. If that happens, it will be a huge blow for me.'

Avijit pondered for a moment before replying. 'On an unofficial basis I am fairly sure that I know who the murderer is, but I have no proof. I told Jamshed that earlier today.'

'Is there a chance that you will be able to obtain that proof soon?' said the inspector.

'Yes, fairly soon. I will need your help,' said Avijit.

'In what way?' said the inspector.

'I would rather not say at this point in time,' said Avijit. 'But you do not have long to wait.'

With that the inspector had to be content. He got up and took his leave.

***

'Brother's Devotion Saves Anahita's Fortune', ran the headline in the *Sentinel* the next day.

This paper has consistently held that Vishwa Jyoti's retreat is bogus. Today's verdict has confirmed our belief. Ardeshir Bilimoria was vindicated today when the district court overturned his sister Anahita's will made in favour of the retreat and upheld his challenge. The court passed stringent remarks on the retreat and its shady activities. Seances, drugs, and preying on innocent women have no place in civilized society. The court has upheld Ardeshir's plea of undue influence and has directed the police to investigate the retreat more thoroughly. Stopping short at pulling up the police for the investigation so far, the court also said that investigation into Anahita's mysterious death needs to conclude speedily. This paper has always maintained that the retreat is behind Anahita's murder. It is time that public-spirited citizens enforce the shutdown of the retreat if the police fail to act.

'Retreat Will Not Go to High Court', said another headline.

The *Daily Voice* interviewed Marjorie, who said, 'The retreat is a place for spiritual activities. We have been unnecessarily dragged into commercial matters. Vishwa Jyotiji has decided that we will not prolong this legal battle any further. We want to rededicate ourselves to taking care of the spiritual needs of our followers'. The paper added, 'The pious hope expressed by the retreat may not be fulfilled. We have heard that many of Vishwa Jyoti's followers have left Mussoorie already and many more are following suit at the time of going to press. We also hear that the police are conducting raids at their retreats in Bombay, Poona, and other cities. The retreat's activities are no longer tenable, and it may just be a matter of time before Vishwa Jyoti and his associates are arrested again. It was a pity that the case against them for molestation came to nought. It is time for the police to do their duty.'

***

'Well! The papers are having a field day, but for once I feel they are justified. These retreat people are vultures,' said Jamshed.

'While all this has been going on, there is one question that I have been meaning to ask you. Why did you not add your name to the case? After all, you also stand to inherit fifty per cent of Anahita's fortune,' said Avijit.

Jamshed paused before answering. 'I have made up my mind on this, Avijit. I do not want a penny of my wife's money. Even if it does come to me, I will donate the entire amount to charity,' said Jamshed emotionally.

Avijit looked at him for a long moment and then got up and put his arm around his friend. 'Your sentiments do you great honour. They also exonerate you from any suspicion that may have occurred that you had done away with Anahita. It is no ordinary person who can just say goodbye to a very large fortune,' said Avijit. 'And now you must excuse me, as I have to make a trunk call,' said Avijit.

'I see,' said Jamshed, 'and may I ask where to?'

'To Poona,' said Avijit as he walked towards the reception and asked the hotel operator to get him an urgent call.

The call was soon over and Avijit walked back to where Jamshed was finishing his breakfast.

'Shall we walk across to the police station? I want to meet Inspector Baluni,' said Avijit.

Jamshed got up and they walked out of the White Palisades Hotel.

'Things are not going well for me,' said the inspector frankly. They had settled down with small glasses of tea in the inspector's room. 'You must have read the press articles. The SP is quite upset as there is now huge pressure to hand over the Anahita murder case and the related matter of the retreat's activities to the CBI.'

'I came to talk to you about that,' said Avijit. 'Matters are moving swiftly now, and I expect that there should be some significant developments in the next few days.'

'I hope so,' said the inspector disconsolately.

'There is something that I need from you,' said Avijit.

The inspector listened attentively as Avijit spoke. He nodded his agreement and said, 'The search warrant is still in force. Let me know the instant you have any word. Here is my telephone number at home.' He handed over a visiting card that had his official and residence numbers on it.

'I need to go to a photographer's shop,' said Avijit.

'There's one opposite Bata,' said Jamshed. They walked up the slope and Avijit went into the photographer's shop saying that he would not take long. He soon came out and told Jamshed, 'I will need to pick up some things from here after an hour.'

'You are not going to tell me anything so we may as well have a nice lunch,' said Jamshed.

They walked into the Maharaja Restaurant and decided to have Chinese food. The simple but delicious meal of sweet corn chicken soup, chow mein, sweet and sour pork, and chilly chicken was washed down with a bottle of Golden Falcon beer. An ice cream and coffee added to the feeling of complete blissfulness.

'Ah! The simple pleasures of life,' said Avijit. 'I must say that Mussoorie has a lot to offer for one who likes food.'

'That being you, of course,' said Jamshed smiling.

'I've always maintained that feeding the little grey cells as Hercule Poirot so picturesquely calls them is the key to being a successful detective,' proclaimed Avijit. Here again he differed with the Great Master, who was known to go for days without food when on an important case.

They sauntered back to the White Palisades Hotel after picking up a small packet from the photographer's shop. A good dinner was followed by a restful night. A telegram arrived the next morning.

PREMISES RAIDED YESTERDAY EVENING STOP BROWN BRIEFCASE DID NOT HAVE DOCUMENTS STOP NOT FOUND IN FLAT ALSO STOP OLD CARETAKER IN CUSTODY VERY ILL STOP YOUNG MAN HAS RUN AWAY STOP DAMLE

Avijit's eyes were gleaming. 'The plot thickens,' he said, rubbing his hands together. Jamshed looked at him but did not ask any questions. It was a slow morning. Avijit was in a state of excitement. He could not sit still but was reluctant to go outside the hotel. Around eleven in the morning, Ardeshir walked into the hotel. He walked up to where Jamshed and Avijit were sitting and sought permission to join them.

'I came to invite both of you for dinner,' said Ardeshir.

'Thank you,' said Avijit. 'When?'

'This evening, if it's not too short a notice,' said Ardeshir apologetically. 'As you may know, the court has ruled in my favour, and I wanted to celebrate. I will probably leave Mussoorie soon, as I need to complete the court paperwork, and set out for Bombay to meet Dr Taraporewala, so I thought it would be wonderful if both of you could join me at Darlington Hall tonight.'

Avijit looked at Jamshed, who nodded. 'Thank you for the invitation. We will be there. What time would you like us to come?'

'Eight o'clock, if that's okay with you,' said Ardeshir. Avijit acquiesced, so they shook hands and Ardeshir left.

***

That evening, before setting off for Darlington Hall, Avijit requested the hotel manager to keep some items in the hotel safe. He had taken them out of the briefcase that was kept in his room. It had a simple lock that could be opened with a generic key.

It was a breezy evening and the clouds had gathered in the valley. As they set out, the first drops of rain fell out of the leaden sky. They were both wearing waterproof boots, and with raincoats and umbrellas, they were well equipped to enjoy the inclement weather. As they walked onto Camel's Back Road, the wind increased and so did the lightning and thunder. The flashes of lightning illuminated the hills as they walked and the houses on the next hill appeared etched in the blinding, bluish light. It was raining in earnest as they passed the Chatri and rounded the bend before Darlington Hall. As they climbed the slope towards the house, the lights went out. Huddled in their raincoats, they knocked on the door. After a while, Agnes answered and let them in. A few candles had been lit, but the house looked shrouded in darkness. They took a few minutes to take off their raincoats and boots and leave their umbrellas to dry in the lobby, after which they walked into the drawing room where they were welcomed by Ardeshir.

'It's a very wild night,' said Ardeshir. He seemed to have gained confidence after the court verdict in his favour.

'When shall we three meet again? In thunder, lightning, or in rain? When the hurly-burly's done, when the battle's lost and won. All hail, Macbeth, that shalt be king hereafter!' declaimed Avijit. He made an ironic bow to Ardeshir.

Ardeshir ignored him, though his face turned a little red. 'I have some rather special whisky. Would you like to try it?'

'Ah, The Macallan!' said Avijit. 'Eighteen years old and cask strength! This is very rare indeed.'

'I have been saving it for a special occasion,' said Ardeshir. He poured out three generous portions into simple glasses. 'I apologize for the wrong kind of glass, but we are a little short in Mussoorie.'

Avijit waved away his apology. 'The whisky tastes just as good in any kind of glass.'

Ardeshir added a touch of water to the glasses and handed them around. Agnes came in with some snacks on a platter that she placed on the coffee table.

'It seems your decision to call Ardeshir was a good one. Unfortunately, Anahita died, but at least the retreat has not been able to get hold of the family wealth,' said Avijit.

'I have always been devoted to the Bilimoria family, sir. I knew that that Marjorie was a bad lot,' said Agnes with some satisfaction.

'You have always remained in touch with Ardeshir,' said Avijit. It was said in a neutral tone.

'Yes, I have brought up Master Ardeshir since the time he was born,' said Agnes proudly.

'This is a great day for you. Congratulations!' said Avijit.

'What are your plans now that you have got your inheritance?' said Jamshed.

'I have a lot of plans. My father had no faith in me, and Dr Taraporewala was always against me,' said Ardeshir. 'I want to set up a global trading business.'

'Like your father,' said Jamshed.

'Yes. I want to be even bigger than he was. Dr Taraporewala will not be able to stop me. I know things about him,' said Ardeshir. There was a crafty look on his face.

'What things?' said Jamshed with a shrug.

'You don't believe me! All of you will have to eat your words,' said Ardeshir.

The level of the Macallan was steadily diminishing. After the first drink, Avijit took over the task of pouring the whisky and Jamshed noticed that Ardeshir's drinks were much bigger than theirs. The cask strength whisky did its work while the wind howled around the house and the storm intensified.

'The whole world has been against me. Only Agnes believed in me and loved me. My sister hated me,' said Ardeshir. He was fast approaching the stage of drunkenness where he'd want to unload all his problems on the people around him, no matter whether they had any interest or not. The door opened and Agnes came in. She looked concerned.

'Baba, it's time we had dinner. It's past ten o'clock,' said Agnes.

Ardeshir was slumped in his seat. He waved a hand in agreement and Agnes went out to bring the food. Dinner was largely in silence. When it was over, Avijit stood up to go, but Agnes stopped him.

'Have some coffee, sir. It will also help Ardeshir baba to get sober,' said Agnes.

Avijit agreed and they went to the drawing room. Agnes came in with the coffee soon afterwards and they sipped in silence. At last, Avijit put down his cup and got up to go.

'Thanks for coming,' said Ardeshir in a slurred voice. He did not get up from the sofa and it was Agnes who saw them out after they had put on their raincoats and gumboots. It was almost eleven o' clock by the time they left Darlington Hall. The storm was blowing itself out and the rain had diminished as they walked back to their hotel. As they entered the hotel lobby, the lights came back on.

'Well, goodnight,' said Jamshed. 'That was quite a boring evening. I think this chap will run through his family wealth in record time.'

'Hopefully not. Anyway, there is no further heir and he will have Dr Taraporewala to contend with. Goodnight,' said Avijit as he turned the key to his room and went in.

Once inside, he put the light on and carefully checked his briefcase. He could tell that it had been opened as the hair that he had lightly pasted on it was askew. He drew on a pair of surgical gloves and opened the briefcase. Some of the things inside were missing. He shut the briefcase and looked around the room. The window opening on the corridor was slightly ajar. It opened when he pushed it. He nodded to himself, well satisfied with the night's work, and went out to the reception. He placed a local call to the inspector's residence and spoke urgently when he picked up.

'Yes. At 6 a.m. I will be there too,' were his final words as he hung up and went back to his room.

21

A Meeting in Sussex

Sir Arthur Conan Doyle
Windlesham Manor
Crowborough
East Sussex, England

25 August 1910

Dear Doyle,

You may have already heard about the murder in Mussoorie of Margaret Maynard-Liddell.

A man who used to be my colleague at the *Frontier* newspaper has written me several letters detailing the circumstances, and I had the opportunity to look around personally on my recent trip to India.

It is a most mystifying case and at first glance looks almost impossible.

I was reading about the excellent defence you had provided for George Edalji and, given our mutual interest in India, was rather hoping that you could take up the case.

Yours sincerely,
Rudyard Kipling

***

Rudyard Kipling Esq.
Bateman's,
Burwash,
East Sussex, England

7 September 1910

Dear Kipling,

I am indeed intrigued by the case. Prior to receiving your letter, I had seen some articles in the press, but as these tend to focus on the more sensational aspects, one tends to discount them. Coincidentally, I have met the lady who met with this unfortunate fate. She was keenly interested in spiritualism and had attended a seance with some others and me in London. I had also introduced her to some people in

India. Poor thing, she was a lost soul. I hope we can do something for her.

If you and Mrs Kipling are free on Saturday, 10 September, it would be nice if you could join us for dinner at Windlesham Manor. The distance is not above sixteen miles, and you can easily drive over in your motor car in half an hour.

We keep country hours at Windlesham, so dinner is served at 6.30 p.m. We will have plenty of time to discuss the case after that.

Your sincerely,
Arthur Conan Doyle

***

Rudyard Kipling was delighted to receive his senior friend's letter. On Saturday, the Kiplings were warmly welcomed at Windlesham Manor, having motored over in less than half an hour as Conan Doyle had predicted.

The ladies withdrew after dinner as they could see that the menfolk were keen to discuss the case. Conan Doyle led his friend to the billiards room, where a fire had been lit. Though it was only September, the weather was blustery, and the warmth of the fire was very welcome. He poured out glasses of brandy and the two men settled down to talk. Their cigars were soon glowing strongly as Kipling handed over the bundle of letters from Charles Harewood to his friend to read. Conan Doyle read steadily for half an hour and then thoughtfully handed the letters back to Kipling.

'I was rather hoping that you could find the time to travel to India and take up the case,' said Kipling. 'I have been there, but it is not the same thing.'

'I would like to, but my other commitments make that impossible at the moment,' said Doyle. 'However, the circumstances are certainly unusual. Unfortunately, the "mystery" of a death in a locked room overpowers logical thought. It's like a stage magician. You get so engrossed in his professional patter that you miss the sleight of hand.'

'You will need to be more explicit,' said Kipling. 'I am all at sea.'

Doyle looked at his friend speculatively and quoted, 'How often have I said to you that when you have eliminated the impossible, whatever remains, however improbable, must be the truth? We know that he did not come through the door, the window, or the chimney. We also know that he could not have been concealed in the room, as there is no concealment possible. Whence, then, did he come?'

Kipling smiled at his friend and finished the quote, 'He came through the hole in the roof. Well, not precisely the hole, but the import is clear enough. I do know my Holmes!'

The two friends sat in silence for a while as they thought about the implications of what they had just discussed.

'The skylight had a small opening. I don't think a grown person could pass through it,' said Kipling in a shaky voice. He murmured, '"Holmes," I said, in a whisper, "a child has done the horrid thing".'

'It was not a child who committed the murder in *The Sign of the Four*, but here I very much fear that that may be the only solution,' said Doyle.

Kipling shuddered as he remembered the child in Mussoorie who had told him about how he liked to climb with ropes. He recounted the incident to Doyle, who nodded slowly.

'The boy must have been told to put something in the woman's mouth,' said Kipling. He looked shocked and horrified.

'It is a sombre yet satisfying moment when your theory appears to be right,' said Doyle. 'The presence of a child was a mathematical certainty, but now it is a real one as well.'

'There was the evidence of the ayah who saw someone running across the roof. It was ignored by the police if I remember correctly,' said Kipling.

'Crucial evidence often is,' said Doyle.

'Another way of looking at it is, who benefits from the crime,' said Kipling at length.

'Miss Levitt on the face of it,' said Doyle. 'However, if you think about it, there could be another possibility.'

Kipling looked at his friend with slowly dawning comprehension. 'I see,' he said at length.

'And the rather unsavoury Mr Dankworth?' said Doyle.

'An instrument?' said Kipling. 'Disposable at that.'

'Perhaps,' said Doyle.

'He must have used the butler's help. Maybe he overplayed his hand demanding more than what the market could withstand,' said Kipling a shade cynically.

'Is it worth propounding this theory to the police?' said Doyle consideringly. 'Perhaps not. There is really no concrete evidence, and the case is already in the high court.'

'I agree with you. This will be dismissed as mere speculation. Well, I must be going. I don't think this mystery is going to be resolved,' said Kipling.

'Maybe a future detective will prove to be shrewder than the Mussoorie Police. Unsolved mysteries are like an itch that must be scratched,' said Doyle.

'Let's leave it at that,' said Kipling as the two men shook hands.

22

Denouement

Avijit knocked loudly on Jamshed's door at five in the morning. It was not dawn yet, but the first streaks of light were lightening the eastern side. He had to knock for quite some time before Jamshed sleepily opened the door. He looked at Avijit in surprise, rubbing the sleep from his eyes. 'Is everything all right?' he said. He then noticed that Avijit was fully dressed and became more alert.

'Get dressed immediately,' said Avijit. Jamshed obeyed and went inside the room. 'Meet me in the lobby at 5.30.'

Jamshed was fully dressed and ready by 5.20. He knew that it was serious business. Avijit was waiting for him in the hotel lobby with two mugs of tea. They drank the tea in silence and left the hotel by 5.30. There was considerably more light by then and some of the early morning traffic, newspaper vendors, and milkmen had already started work. It was a dewy morning. The storm had left a lot of debris in its wake. There were leaves and paper strewn all over the road awaiting the sweepers who would start work later in the morning. They walked rapidly down Mall Road and on to Camel's Back Road. Jamshed did not ask any questions until they began the short ascent to Darlington Hall. It was then that he saw the police jeep parked unobtrusively a little way away from the house. The inspector and four policemen armed with rifles were awaiting their arrival on the main road. Avijit shook hands with the inspector and gestured to them to carry on with their work. The police party climbed up to Darlington Hall and surrounded the property while the inspector went around to the kitchen window on the hillside of the house. He knocked softly on the window and the Pahari cleaning maid came to the window to see who it was. The inspector spoke to her softly in Garhwali and she went out of the kitchen and opened the back door that led to the servant's quarters. The inspector, a constable, Avijit, and Jamshed quietly entered the house. The inspector asked the maid to knock on Agnes's door. After a while when Agnes opened the door, the inspector walked in authoritatively and said, 'You are under arrest.' The Pahari maid and Avijit were right behind him. The inspector handcuffed Agnes and led her out to the drawing room. He left her there in charge of an armed guard and joined Avijit, who had remained in her room.

Meanwhile, the constable along with Jamshed had gone upstairs and had repeated the process at Ardeshir's door. It was more difficult to wake him up as he was in a drunken stupor, but they finally managed, and the constable put the handcuffs on him as well. He was taken to the morning room with an armed guard to look after him.

'What are we looking for?' said the inspector.

'A couple of photographs and a roll of film,' said Avijit.

The search did not take long. Obviously, Agnes had not anticipated that the police raid would take place so soon. All the items were kept in her bedside drawer.

Agnes and Ardeshir had been sent to the police station after their statements had been recorded. Ardeshir appeared to be completely demoralized.

'It's only a matter of time before we extract a complete confession from him,' said the inspector.

The three of them were sitting in the morning room with the sunlight streaming in. The Pahari maid had provided tea and the driver of the police jeep had fetched poori sabzi and jalebis for their breakfast from the Mussoorie Library. There was an expectant silence as they waited for Avijit to explain what he had done.

'Their first mistake was placing the sleeping powders in the box beside Anahita's bedside table,' said Avijit.

The inspector hit his head with his hand. 'I could see that there was something suspicious about the powders, but I could not figure out whether the box was empty in the morning or not.'

'That's because you had not seen it for yourself, Inspector. If you recall, I stayed behind in Anahita's room for a while just after her death. I had seen for myself that the box was empty at that time. When you found the powder there later, it was obvious that someone in the house must have put it there,' said Avijit.

'But why?' said Jamshed. 'There was really no reason for them to put the powder in the box.'

'I think it was only to create a greater sense of mystery. A little childish perhaps, but many criminals think like that,' said Avijit.

'Please start at the beginning, sir,' requested the inspector.

'It started with Agnes calling Ardeshir to Mussoorie,' said Avijit. 'If you look at the sequence of events, you will find that Anahita's behaviour changed after a point in time. She started becoming more remote and disconnected from the retreat. Clearly, it must have been something that she saw or heard while she was there. It is fair to assume that Agnes may have been telling the truth—that Anahita did refer to Vishwa Jyoti as a rapist. That could be the reason why she started disassociating herself from the retreat.'

'We do not have any proof of this,' said the inspector thoughtfully. 'It would have been very helpful in nailing down the disreputable activities of Vishwa Jyoti.'

'True, but that is a separate matter. At this point, we are focusing on Anahita's murder,' said Avijit.

The inspector nodded. 'What happened next?'

'There was a change in Anahita's behaviour. I can only surmise, but her lethargy and tiredness started increasing. Marjorie was also openly giving her the sleeping powder. I think the retreat may have become worried that Anahita and her fortune may slip through their hands. They may have accelerated their programme to render her more docile.'

'With what objective?' said Jamshed.

'That is clear enough. They wanted her to sign a will in favour of the retreat. It is possible that she signed this without being in full possession of her senses,' said Avijit.

'But the witnesses?' said the inspector.

'They are a doctor and a lawyer, both of whom are indebted to the retreat. In fact, that is the same doctor who prescribed the sleeping powder for Anahita. They could have signed at any time, not necessarily at the time that Anahita signed the document,' said Avijit. 'In any case, the will was kept at the retreat.'

'I am guessing here, but I think Agnes may have actually seen the will or maybe a document being signed. That could have triggered the call to Ardeshir,' said Avijit.

'What do you think was the retreat's objective of getting Anahita to sign the will?' said the inspector.

Avijit looked grave. 'There are a number of women who have signed a will in favour of the retreat, Inspector. Many of them died subsequently. It is not hard to see the connection. We do not have proof, but now that a modus operandi seems to be emerging, it may be possible to find some evidence. Bajwa and Marjorie are very accomplished frauds and possibly murderers.'

'What did Agnes want Ardeshir to do?' said Jamshed.

'We are getting into the realm of conjecture here. They knew that Anahita had written a will in favour of the retreat. If Anahita died, the retreat would've been the obvious suspect. It would have been ideal if she had died while Marjorie was still living at Darlington Hall, but Anahita forced their hand by throwing Marjorie out. They had to advance their plans and do away with Anahita that same night, hoping that suspicion would fall on the retreat, especially since the sleeping powders were being given by Marjorie. It could also be considered a natural death—an accidental overdose by Anahita herself,' said Avijit.

'But the will was in favour of the retreat. Agnes and Ardeshir would have nothing to benefit from her death,' said Jamshed.

'I think they were fairly sure that the will would be overturned. There are a number of precedents for it,' said the inspector.

'I am not clear why Agnes was so much in favour of Ardeshir. After all, she was employed by Anahita,' said Jamshed.

The inspector nodded. 'Yes, why?'

'Agnes is Ardeshir's mother,' said Avijit.

'What!' said the inspector and Jamshed in unison.

'Yes,' said Avijit with a smile. 'I found two birth certificates in Ardeshir's house. One was in his name giving his parents' names as Bahram and Arnavaz Bilimoria. But there was another one too, which was dated a few days earlier. A male child had been born to Agnes De Mello. The child's name was not recorded, but the father's name is shown as Bahram Bilimoria. We know that Agnes had come as a maid into the Bilimoria household some time before Ardeshir was born. She delivered a male child a few days before Arnavaz Bilimoria also delivered a boy. Arnavaz died in childbirth, and it is quite possible that her child died too. Bahram probably had an affair with Agnes, and she became pregnant as a result. She may have been sent away before her child was born, but Bahram must have sensed an opportunity for perpetuating his family name and called her back.'

'So, he switched the children?' said Jamshed.

'It certainly seems like it. What else can explain Agnes's devotion to Ardeshir? She has been in touch with him throughout,' said Avijit. 'Look at this picture.' He showed them the picture of Agnes sitting on a chair holding a new-born baby with Bahram standing alongside. It certainly looked like a family picture.

'You haven't told us how the murder was committed,' said the inspector.

'Ah that! Indeed, a clever ploy,' said Avijit with a chuckle. 'I have reconstructed the crime as follows. One dose of

Seconal was given to Anahita in the last cup of coffee that she had had that evening. If you recall, she was very sleepy and could barely keep her eyes open at dinner. She went up early and when Agnes came up with her nightly glass of milk, she appeared to be already asleep. She left the glass of milk on her bedside table. That glass had a lethal dose of Seconal when coupled with the drug Anahita had already consumed. Agnes said that she went out of the room leaving the door unlocked. But that is not what happened. She picked up the key and locked the door from outside, taking the key with her.'

The inspector and Jamshed were listening with rapt attention. 'But Anahita had not drunk her milk as she was asleep,' said Jamshed.

Avijit nodded. 'Yes, she did not drink the milk at that time. Do you know why?'

'Why?' said the inspector.

'Because then there would not have been any need for the loud crash that happened in the night,' said Avijit. He sat back in his chair and watched the growing light of understanding dawning on the inspector's face.

'I see!' said the inspector.

Avijit smiled and said, 'Precisely.'

'Well, I don't understand,' said Jamshed plaintively. 'Please explain in plain words.'

'If you recall, there was a loud crash that night a little after the household had settled down. We were told that Ardeshir had knocked over his bedside table while getting up to go to the bathroom. I have checked the table that had fallen over. It is a very heavy table placed in a corner. It is impossible that it could have been knocked over by accident. No, it was deliberately done by Ardeshir with the sole objective of waking up Anahita. Only a thin wall separates the two rooms and the bedside table is almost next to Anahita's bed. The sound was loud enough for her to wake up and in her fuddled state, she saw the glass of milk lying by her on the table and drank it,' said Avijit.

'That's ingenious, but a bit hit or miss,' said Jamshed.

'Indeed. But there was a reasonable probability of it happening. They may have had a backup plan of forcing Anahita to drink the milk somehow, but it was not required,' said Avijit.

'What happened afterwards?' said the inspector.

'Do you recall that the cleaning maid said that she heard some footsteps after the crash? That was Agnes carrying up another glass with some milk at the bottom. She opened the door of Anahita's room, went in, and wrapped the dead woman's right hand around the glass to register her fingerprints. She then placed this glass on the table and picked up the one that had the narcotic. She later washed that glass and put it back in the kitchen later that morning. As she left Anahita's room, she locked the door and kept the key with her. It was not possible to make out that the door had not been locked from the inside,' said Avijit.

'A perfectly dressed-up crime scene!' said the inspector.

'What followed was as per their script. When Anahita did not wake up, Ardeshir decided to have the door broken down. This was done and the last person to enter was Agnes. She told the cleaning maid to get on with her work of cleaning Ardeshir's room and then discreetly kept the room key on the dresser, where the police discovered it when they came in. She also dropped the bolt fitting on the floor that Ardeshir had broken earlier, giving the impression that the door bolt had broken when the door was forced open. It automatically created the illusion of a locked and bolted room and a mysterious death when the murder was fairly simple,' said Avijit.

There was a contemplative silence as they digested Avijit's words.

'How do you prove all this?' said Jamshed.

As if on cue, a constable entered the room and requested permission to speak to the inspector. He told him to go ahead.

'Sir, we have arrested the burglar,' said the constable.

'Where was he found?' said the inspector.

'Sir, as per your instructions, we had men in plainclothes watching the White Palisades Hotel last evening. It was raining heavily when they left the hotel,' said the constable gesturing towards Avijit and Jamshed. 'We kept up the vigil and sure enough at around ten o'clock, we saw a man who had entered the hotel premises on the ground floor where the Ajax Cinema is. He climbed up to the first floor where the hotel rooms are located by a drainpipe. He went to Room No. 3 and tried the door. He found it locked, so he tried the window, which was open. He went in and came out after about ten minutes through the same window. It was quite dark, so we could not see his face, but we followed him,' said the constable.

'Where did he go?' said the inspector.

'He went to Darlington Hall. We followed him there. He went in after they had come out. It was exactly 11.10. He stayed inside for about fifteen minutes and then came out of the back door. As it turns out, he is the gardener who works here. He has been in his quarters since then. Two of our men have been here the whole night watching him. We saw you coming at six in the morning and we waited as per your instructions till 7.30 before arresting him. A constable has been sitting inside his quarters with him since six,' said the constable.

'Shabash! You have done well. Please bring the man in,' said the inspector.

The gardener was brought in in handcuffs. He looked terrified and was only too willing to tell his story. Agnes had apparently found him stealing some things from the house and had threatened to tell the police. He agreed to commit the burglary as he was scared. He had been told what to steal from the room and nothing else. He had been paid a thousand rupees for the work. That was all that he knew. The inspector told the constable to take him to the police station and they left soon afterwards.

'Well, that was a good piece of work. What a brilliant set-up! Hats off, Avijit. I guess your visit to the photography shop was to create a dummy packet with copies of the photographs and the roll of film that would be substituted for the real ones,' said Jamshed admiringly.

'And the real ones were safely stored in the hotel safe,' said Avijit.

'Brilliant! You are to be congratulated,' said the inspector.

'There is one last link. Ardeshir's servant had given me a receipt from a medical store in his name when I told him that I was sick. By sheer luck, it was a receipt for a month's supply of Seconal sold to Ardeshir. The date was just the day before he left for Mussoorie,' said Avijit.

'Bravo! This is just terrific! I think we should be able to nail these two down with all the evidence we have. It is circumstantial, but I think we have enough,' said the inspector.

'Lean on Ardeshir and keep him away from Agnes. He is by far the weaker of the two. I think you will have a confession soon,' said Avijit.

They shook hands and left Darlington Hall. The case was complete.

Epilogue

Conan Doyle never forgot about the Mussoorie murder. A few years later at a literary event in London, during the First World War, he met a young woman who told him that she wanted to write a murder mystery.

'Well, that should be easy enough,' said Doyle jovially.

'The whole problem is that I am unable to come up with a really intriguing plot,' confessed the woman.

'Well, if you are really keen, I can offer you the story of a murder that has never been solved,' said Doyle.

'Oh please! That would be wonderful! May I meet you again?' said the woman.

'Why not now? I have an hour to kill and there is a Lyon's Café just round the corner,' said Doyle.

Over the next hour, Doyle told the young woman about the Mussoorie murder and the most puzzling aspect of how the crime was committed in a room locked and bolted from the inside.

'That is a really intriguing story!' exclaimed the woman.

'Well, the idea's yours now. I hope you make a go of it,' said Doyle.

A few years later, after the war had ended, the young woman's first novel, *The Mysterious Affair at Styles*, was published. It featured the death of a woman in a room locked and bolted from inside and introduced a detective, Hercule Poirot, who would in time become as famous as Sherlock Holmes.

The young woman's name was Agatha Christie. Or so claimed some of the literary event's attendees later in time.

***

'I wonder if there really was a link with the 1909 murder at the Lexton Plaza,' said Jamshed idly.

The two friends were in a taxi on their way to Dehradun. The inspector had come to see them off at the Picture Palace bus stand, and after an affectionate farewell, they were soon on their way to catch the Mussoorie Express to Delhi.

Avijit smiled at his friend. 'There's something I haven't told anybody yet.'

'I'm all ears,' said Jamshed.

'I found a small notebook amongst the other papers when I had gone to Ardeshir's house in Poona. It was an old notebook with yellowing pages,' said Avijit. He felt in his coat pocket and took out a small, leather-bound notebook. He opened it and showed it to Jamshed, who looked at it closely.

'That's strange. The script looks like Hindi, but I am unable to make head or tail of what is written,' said Jamshed.

Avijit chuckled. 'I had the same problem until on a hunch I showed it to Pandit Madhur Kaul.'

'You mean the old painter who has a studio near the Standard Skating Rink? He's Kashmiri, isn't he?' said Jamshed.

'Precisely. The script turned out to be the Sharada script. It was used by Kashmiri Pandits and was fairly widespread in Himachal Pradesh too,' said Avijit. 'Panditji was able to identify the script and with some difficulty managed to read what was written in the notebook. He translated it at my request, and I have the English translation here with me.'

Jamshed took the loose papers from him and began to read. The twisting and turning of the taxi as it traversed the steep road down towards Dehradun made the task more difficult, but he persisted, planting his feet firmly on the floor of the taxi.

Ashok, my son,

I write this after it is all over. What I have done is between me and my God. I have sinned deeply, but there is no recourse on earth. I did it only for you, my son! So that you could make a life for yourself better than what we have had here.

'Who is writing this? What connection does it have with this case?' said Jamshed with a puzzled frown.

'Read on. The connection will become clear and so will the writer's identity,' said Avijit.

I had to leave Jaramogi soon after your mother died. I was in the service of the pujari. But, my son, human beings are frail and greedy, and I was tempted. The pujari was a good man. He suspected that I was stealing from the offerings made by devotees at the temple but could not prove it. One day, he searched my room in the temple premises and found the money hidden below the floorboards. He taxed me with it and said that he would give me up to the police. I pleaded with him, but he was adamant. In the heat of the moment, I picked up a piece of firewood that was lying in a heap in the room. I hit him on the head with it. I hit him again and again until his head was disfigured. He was dead.

You walked in through the door just then. I ran to you and gathered you in my arms. I led you outside so that you might not see the body. You were just four, my son! How could I let you see what I had done? I gathered up a few belongings and the money that I had stolen, and we left the same day. I had no idea where we were going. I knew the jungles better than most people and so we walked the whole night avoiding the road. In the daytime, we slept in the shade of a tree. Luckily, it was summer, so it was possible to sleep outside. In the evening, I walked to a nearby town and got some food. It was a miracle that we did not get caught. After almost a week, we reached Ambala. We went to the railway station as I had resolved to catch the first train that came our way. We had just finished eating pooris when a train came in. It was coming from Lahore and going to Dehradun. I bought tickets and we spent the night in a crowded compartment. Dehradun was the biggest town that I had ever seen. I got a job soon as a waiter in a restaurant. They were looking for a kitchen assistant, but when the malik realized that I could read and write, he decided to make me a waiter. I used to look for a better job all the time. It was only the next year that a waiter's job was advertised at the Lexton Plaza Hotel in Mussoorie. I bought a new set of clothes and went up to Mussoorie for the interview. I got the job and soon afterwards, I was promoted as a room butler. The years passed and I met many memsahibs and gora sahibs during that job. They barely took any notice of me.

They had reached close to Dehradun as Jamshed looked up from his reading. He was lost in thought as the taxi turned right on the bypass. There was a silence as the car drove through the suburbs of Dehradun towards the clock tower. Avijit told the driver to stop at the Careton Restaurant and the two friends got off to stretch their legs and have dinner before catching their train to Delhi.

Dankworth sahib was different from the other gora sahibs. I was his special favourite as I was able to get the best ganja and hashish for him. He used to come to my room, and we used to smoke many chillums together. I had gone back to my old ways of stealing money from the hotel guests but never in such large amounts so as to avoid getting caught.

There were still three hours for the train's departure, so Jamshed had resumed reading after their drinks had been served in the restaurant. The waiter came up as he was reading and informed Avijit that there was a telephone call for him.

'For me? How would anybody know that I am here,' said Avijit in a surprised voice.

'It's the police, sir. Inspector Baluni from Mussoorie,' said the waiter.

'Oh, I see. I will come at once,' said Avijit.

One day, Dankworth sahib caught me in the act. He was having an affair with a married memsahib whose husband was still in the plains. He had walked into her room one afternoon to wait for her while I was rifling her purse. He came quietly from behind and held my hand in a surprisingly strong grip. He put his finger on his lips and gestured to me to leave the room.

From then onwards, we were partners. He was very good at getting to know memsahibs and was able to find out exactly where they kept their money. We stole small amounts, and nobody complained. One day, in August 1909, he came to my room in a state of great excitement. He asked me if I wanted to make a lot of money. Of course, I said yes! Then he told me what had to be done and my blood ran cold. We discussed the plan through the night smoking many chillums while you slept. You were to have a key role in the plan, and I was not happy. I did not want my son to be like me. But Dankworth sahib was very persuasive. He threatened me with exposure too and only laughed when I said that I would expose him too. Who would believe the word of a poor native over a white man? I asked him who was behind the whole plan, but he said nothing.

I was the butler for Margaret memsahib's suite. She had to be killed. That was what Dankworth sahib told me. She was to die in such a way that nobody would be able to ever find out who killed her and how. He was an intelligent man, but it was I who eventually suggested how it could be accomplished.

Forgive me, my son! It was I who set you on the path of crime. But you did not even know what you did.

Margaret memsahib was in the habit of having a glass of milk at night. On the day of the murder, I brought her the milk as usual but had mixed in a packet of powder that Dankworth sahib gave me. He assured me that it was only a mild sleeping potion so that she would sleep soundly. I believed him. I had to. I kept insisting on meeting the real malik, as I was not convinced that this whole plan was only thought of by Dankworth sahib. He kept refusing and finally gave me fifty rupees as an advance to ensure that I did what he wanted. I thought he was lying, but I had no way of refusing to do what he wanted. The die was cast!

I woke you up at midnight. It was a dark night, as there were clouds covering the moon. Luckily, it was not raining as the roof would have been much more slippery. I carefully explained what you had to do. You were only ten years old, but your understanding was that of a grown man. We made our way stealthily over the roof to Margaret memsahib's room. I gave you a glass with a little milk remaining at the bottom. I tied the rope around your waist and opened the skylight. There was just enough space for you to go through. I let you down by the rope. It was long enough to reach into the bedroom. After a short while, you tugged on the rope, and I pulled you back to the roof. I carefully closed the skylight and untied the rope around your waist. You gave me the glass which you had picked up from the bedside table and we crept back across the roof to the staff quarters. As we were moving, the clouds cleared, and the moon came out. I looked around and thought I saw a woman in a white sari on the veranda of the wing opposite. In that instant, the clouds covered the moon again and soon we were in my quarters. You told me that Margaret memsahib was sleeping on her back and that you had put the candy in her mouth as you had been told. She did not move when you did it and you picked up the glass, leaving the other one behind, and left the room. I rinsed out the glass and we went to sleep.

Little remains to be told. Dankworth sahib gave me the money soon afterwards. It was more than I could earn in five years. I asked him to help to get you into an English school now that I had the money to pay for it.

I am writing this so that you know the truth, my son. I am getting old now and may die soon. This letter is written in our ancestral language, and you may not be able to read it. Perhaps that is best. It is not an honourable legacy that I leave behind for you.

Your father,
Rajesh

It was 8 p.m. by the time Jamshed finished reading the letter. He pushed it aside with a shudder. 'The mind boggles.

For a father to have made his ten-year-old son commit such a heinous crime is horrible,' said Jamshed. 'Maybe there was another person behind the scenes, the "malik", as Rajesh calls him, but we will never know for sure. As such, it is difficult to see what the motive would be for a small-time crook like Orson Dankworth to commit such a murder on his own. What happened to him afterwards?'

'Nobody knows. He apparently disappeared from what I have been able to find out,' said Avijit.

'I see. Maybe he fell out with the malik, whoever he was,' said Jamshed.

'Possibly,' said Avijit.

'I presume that Rajesh's son Ashok is the same person who was Ardeshir's manservant.'

'Yes. He was grievously ill when he was arrested. In fact, I have just received information from Inspector Baluni that he has died in jail but not before he made a full confession. He was hand in glove with Agnes and Ardeshir and knew that Ardeshir was Agnes's son. When matters came to a head and the only course of action was to get rid of Anahita, it was he who gave them the idea of an unsolvable murder in a locked room,' said Avijit. 'He was picked up by Bahram when he had taken his pregnant wife to Mussoorie before Anahita was born. He then became an indispensable member of their household.'

'So, his confession also nails down the guilt of Agnes and Ardeshir,' said Jamshed.

'Yes. We can now honestly say that the case is closed,' said Avijit.

'It is a great relief to know that Anahita's death has not gone unavenged. I hope that Margaret's soul will also find comfort from what you have unravelled,' said Jamshed.

'Amen to that. Come, it is time to leave for the station,' said Avijit.

They were soon comfortably settled in their air-conditioned compartment and the train had started on its overnight journey to Delhi.

'What do you wish to do now?' said Avijit.

'I have been away from my work for far too long. I will go to Bombay first, as Dr Taraporewala wants me to continue as the managing director for the business. I did tell him that I did not want the money, but he was insistent that I continue nonetheless as a professional. Later, I may go back to London,' said Jamshed. 'This has been a sad as well as an eventful time for me.'

'It has indeed. Work is the only anodyne, my friend,' said Avijit.

'Where will you go?' said Jamshed.

'I may go to Poona. Inspector Damle has called and there could be an interesting case coming up out there,' said Avijit.

Jamshed laughed. 'You have let Inspector Baluni take all the credit in Mussoorie. Are you intending to become the deus ex machina for the Indian police?'

'It's not a bad thought,' said Avijit as he smiled at his friend.

Author's Note

The true story of an unsolved murder of a British lady in a locked room in a prominent hotel in Mussoorie in the early twentieth century generated a lot of speculation and garnered much attention. Rudyard Kipling's interest and his attempt to involve Arthur Conan Doyle is well known and a matter of record.

What is more speculative is whether Agatha Christie was inspired by the events at Mussoorie for writing her first book, *The Mysterious Affair at Styles*. She was a young woman when the murder occurred and her book was published a few years later, in 1920. The circumstances were undoubtedly similar, and Agatha Christie suggested an ingenious technical explanation for how the murder was perpetrated in a locked room. Indian sources tend to emphasize the linkage[1] but Agatha Christie's own website[2] and other reference material make no mention of it.

Anahita Bilimoria's murder sixty years later is entirely fictional, as is the link between the two events. Suffice it to say that readers around the world love a juicy murder mystery, replete with clues, incisive detectives, and a suitably awestruck Watson for every Holmes.

In the fond hope that this volume may find its humble place in that hallowed pantheon.

End Notes

1 Apparently, Rudyard Kipling had written to Arthur Conan Doyle, urging him to write a story about a 'murder by suggestion'. Though Conan Doyle never visited to investigate, he allegedly mentioned it to Agatha Christie and the detective story, *The Mysterious Affair at Styles*, was the result, according to some researchers.
2 https://www.agathachristie.com/

Acknowledgements

There are several people who have played an important role in the creation of this book. Starting with my father, Anand Roop Bhatnagar, who loved reading and had an eclectic collection of books. Even as children we voraciously devoured his volumes of classic detective fiction. Though he passed away when we were very young, he always lived on through these books. My mother, Sudha, was a teacher of English literature and her love for words and facility of expression has stood me in good stead in my writing endeavours. My sister Jyotsna Raj, too, furthered the cause and introduced me to several detective-fiction writers. And thus was born a never-ending love affair with Sherlock Holmes, Hercule Poirot, Miss Marple, Father Brown, Lord Peter Wimsey, and a galaxy of stars from the golden age of detective fiction.

The juxtaposition of detective fiction with my other love, Mussoorie, was spearheaded by my literary agent, Suhail Mathur, the dynamic and affable head of the Book Bakers. The idea for this book emerged in a discussion with him in Delhi, and as I got into the narrative, I realized how right he had been to suggest this fortunate confluence. I would also like to acknowledge my debt of gratitude to Ruskin Bond, the doyen of writers from Mussoorie. His summation of the early twentieth-century murder at a hotel in Mussoorie was invaluable as I developed the plot for this novel. Apart from that, Bond's love for the mountains and the charming elegance of his writing has always been an inspiration for me.

I would like to thank Shantanu Ray Chaudhuri of Om Books International for believing in my work and Sumeet Kaur, my wonderful editor, whose painstaking and brilliant editing has added a new dimension to the book. I would also like to acknowledge Soumya Duggal, whose incisive and relevant suggestions have been of immense value.

My wife, Devi, has been the sounding board for all my ideas ever since I embarked on this journey. Her incisive logic and crystal-clear intellect have helped me clarify my thoughts at every step of the way. My daughters, Priya and Anuradha, were equally helpful with their feedback. My friends Rahul Kansal, Ranjan Kaul, and Anurag Bisaria saw early versions of my work and their suggestions have immensely helped in shaping the final narrative.